W9-AXK-613

CRASH LANDING!

Moonstalker was directly over the lunar crater that was home to the alien object the crew had discovered. On the video screen, Tom could see something atop the strange artifact begin to move.

Suddenly the copilot spoke. "We're getting a transmission. No! It's a burst of static!"

Alarms shrieked as the control board went wild. "It's an electromagnetic pulse," Tom corrected him. "And it's going to destroy our computer controls."

"It's over for all of us." Captain Nelson's voice was hoarse. "That pulse did in four of our five computers, and we need two computers to fly this bird."

"Now we can't control the rockets," Tom said. "The machine we have left will only maintain the environmental equipment and keep us alive."

The copilot's voice was as cold as space itself. "But it won't keep us flying. Our orbit is degrading—we're going to crash into the Moon!"

Books in the Tom Swift® Series

#1 THE BLACK DRAGON
#2 THE NEGATIVE ZONE
#3 CYBORG KICKBOXER
#4 THE DNA DISASTER
#5 MONSTER MACHINE
#6 AQUATECH WARRIORS
#7 MOONSTALKER

Available from ARCHWAY Paperbacks

Most Archway Paperbacks are available at special quantity discounts for bulk purchases for sales promotions, premiums or fund raising. Special books or book excerpts can also be created to fit specific needs.

For details write the office of the Vice President of Special Markets, Pocket Books, 1230 Avenue of the Americas, New York, New York 10020.

TOM SWIFT 7
MOONSTALKER

VICTOR APPLETON

AN ARCHWAY PAPERBACK
Published by POCKET BOOKS
New York London Toronto Sydney Tokyo Singapore

This book is a work of fiction. Names, characters, places and
incidents are either the product of the author's imagination or
are used fictitiously. Any resemblance to actual events or locales
or persons, living or dead, is entirely coincidental.

AN ARCHWAY PAPERBACK *Original*

An Archway Paperback published by
POCKET BOOKS, a division of Simon & Schuster Inc.
1230 Avenue of the Americas, New York, NY 10020

Copyright © 1992 by Simon & Schuster Inc.

Produced by Byron Preiss Visual Publications, Inc.

All rights reserved, including the right to reproduce
this book or portions thereof in any form whatsoever.
For information address Pocket Books, 1230 Avenue
of the Americas, New York, NY 10020

ISBN: 0-671-75645-1

First Archway Paperback printing February 1992

10 9 8 7 6 5 4 3 2 1

TOM SWIFT, AN ARCHWAY PAPERBACK and colophon
are registered trademarks of Simon & Schuster Inc.

Cover art by Carla Sormanti

Printed in the U.S.A.

IL 6+

MOONSTALKER

1

"TONIGHT WE PUT A NEW STAR IN THE SKY."
Tom Swift turned his blue eyes to a power
coupling, ignoring the stare of the young
woman standing beside him.

As a young inventor, he was used to the
kind of look he was getting. This is no ordinary teenager, Tom interpreted that slightly
nervous gaze. This is a nut.

He looked up, a smile on his lean, handsome face. The young woman's curly red hair
brushed her freckled cheeks as her eyes took
in the high-tech gear laid out around the observatory floor.

At least she wasn't running off, calling for
a straitjacket. "If you're making your own
star, Mr. Swift, what do you need our tele-

1

scope for?" The young woman anxiously fingered the University of California ID clipped to her jacket. The card identified her as Alison McVeigh, a student research assistant at the San Damian campus observatory.

"Do me a favor," Tom said, laughing. "Call me Tom. When people say 'Mr. Swift,' I keep looking around for my father."

Tom's father worked on the cutting edge of science and technology. His genius had produced an organization, Swift Enterprises, at the top of the research field. Tom's own genius had made a mark developing new technologies, and he hoped for another breakthrough with the equipment he'd be testing soon.

"Okay, Mr.—ah, Tom. But then, do *me* a favor. Tell me what's going on here—really."

Tom stared. "No one told you anything about this project?"

"Dr. Hobart just asked for a volunteer to operate old Number Two here at the observatory." Her green eyes went to the big, cannonlike tube of the telescope, aimed through the slit in the concrete dome above. The floor was crowded with Tom's experimental setup, including a long, thin box with red letters on its housing: Danger—High-Power Laser.

"Maybe I shouldn't tell you," the girl said, "but the Astronomy Department considers this 'scope hopelessly obsolete. It was top of the line when it was first built. But nowadays, with the glare and the haze from Los Angeles— well, all it's good for is to teach people how to aim a large 'scope. You can't do serious research with it."

"So the university was willing to let me use it. Ah, what can I call you, anyway?" Tom asked.

Color crept over the young woman's high cheekbones. "My friends call me Allie."

"Well, Allie, you've pointed out a major problem for a lot of telescopes these days. What I'm working on may help keep them useful."

"But what are you going to *do?*" Allie asked.

Tom finished the power hookup and gave the laser a cheerful pat. "I'm going to make a new star, by firing this into the sky."

The pretty young woman's jaw dropped. "Is this—are *you*—for real?"

"Trust me, it's not as bizarre as it sounds. What's your biggest problem as an astronomer?"

"I'm just a student," Allie pointed out.

"Okay, student, what's the major problem with Earth-based astronomy?"

"The atmosphere," Allie answered promptly. "Turbulent air does more than make stars twinkle. It blurs the light that comes down to

3

our telescopes." She grinned. "We have a little saying: Twinkle, twinkle, little star. Are my readings off *that* far?"

"What if, no matter where you turned your telescope, you had a guide star to help you tune out those light distortions?" Tom asked.

"Sounds great, if we had one," Allie replied.

"Well, that's what I'm trying to create. This optical hookup lets me fire my laser through your telescope, throwing a tight beam of blue light five miles up. The laser beam reflects off oxygen and nitrogen atoms in the upper atmosphere, forming what looks like a blue star to the telescope."

Allie nodded. "I understand. But what are you doing with this other equipment?"

Tom pointed to one box. "This is a sensor and computer rig. It examines what the telescope sees. Since it already has the data on the guide star, it can determine how the atmosphere is distorting the starlight. That information goes to this gizmo, a deformable mirror."

"Sounds like a fun house," Allie said.

Tom shook his head. "This mirror bends by precise computer control. That controlled warping removes any distortions in the light entering the telescope. Add a good infrared camera, and in theory, you have a telescope that can capture images in invisible light and even from far away, dimly glowing celestial objects. In other words, you've got a much more powerful 'scope."

Allie looked at Tom's equipment with new respect. "How much more powerful?"

"By my calculations, this telescope would have the image quality of a 'scope about ten times larger."

Now Allie stared in shock. "That's stronger than our number one telescope." She thought for a second. "It's even better than the biggest scope in America, the one on Mount Palomar."

"*If* it works," Tom quickly pointed out. "Tonight, though, we'll test only the laser connection and aiming."

Allie smiled. "Well, I'm glad to be on your team." She went to a computer console set against one wall of the observatory and flipped a few switches. A large TV monitor came to life, showing what the telescope was "seeing."

"So what do you need, a nice dark patch of sky?" Allie's fingers darted over a computer keyboard. With the sound of giant gears slowly grinding, the snout of the telescope ponderously swung around. The TV monitor now showed a fairly blank section of night sky.

Tom turned from the screen. "Perfect. Now to tune up the laser." He flicked a switch on his portable control console, and the observatory filled with a low-frequency hum. He turned a dial, and the humming grew faster, rising in pitch until it became a shrill whine. "Now!" Tom said, thrusting at a button.

Above them, a brilliant burst of blue light flew from the telescope. On the TV monitor, a twinkling blue dot suddenly appeared in the middle of the picture. Allie McVeigh stared in awe. "It looks just like a star! If I hadn't seen this—"

Tom cut her off abruptly, staring at the screen. "What's that?" he asked. A tiny speck of white moved against the dark background of space.

Allie squinted her green eyes. "A satellite? But it's moving in retrograde orbit—opposite to the way most satellites circle the Earth." She blinked. "And I picked this part of the sky because there's supposed to be nothing up there."

"Too far up to be a passing plane," Tom said. "Can you focus on it?"

Allie's fingers flew over the keyboard. The view shrank, but the moving speck grew, showing regular lines. "A box?" She frowned as she focused in, and the cubical shape grew sharper.

"It's not so high up, apparently following a decaying orbit, and coming closer and closer to Earth. Friction with the atmosphere will probably burn it up before it reaches the ground." Allie stared at the puzzling image. "Maybe it's an old satellite from the sixties."

"Whatever it is, I'd like a better look at it." Tom had already turned to his other equipment and was hooking it into the cables attached to the telescope. "I wasn't going to test the whole system tonight, but why not?"

In moments he had everything connected, while Allie adjusted the telescope to follow the mysterious object in the sky.

The hum and whine followed as Tom powered up the laser. Then he fired. Again a blue dot appeared in the middle of the screen. But after a few seconds, its twinkle disappeared as the computer filtered out the atmospheric disturbance. Everything else on the screen was much sharper, including the image of the cube.

The edges of the strange box were now straight and clear. Instead of a vague impression of mere brightness, they could see that the side facing them shone like polished stone, and there was something carved into the gleaming surface.

"What does it say?" Allie squinted in confusion, trying to make out the spidery carving.

"That's not the English alphabet," Tom said, looking just as hard. "And those aren't Russian or Arabic letters either."

"Could it be Chinese, maybe? Japanese?" Allie suggested.

Tom shook his head. "I'm familiar enough with the letter forms of those languages—and some others—to be able to recognize something. And I don't."

"Then what *is* it?" Allie sounded deeply uneasy.

Tom glanced at her. "I'd better get the cameras on-line. Whatever that message is, it's not written in any language used on Earth."

2

TOM SWIFT LOADED THE OPTICAL SYSTEM'S still camera with infrared film. Shot after shot clicked off automatically as he stared at the puzzling picture on the screen.

Alison McVeigh's green eyes also darted to the strange body as she plotted its orbital path. "Right now, the object is about seven hundred miles up, but the orbit's low point will bring the thing much closer to earth."

Tom noticed that Allie resolutely called the orbiting enigma an object or thing. He went on shooting pictures as long as the strange body stayed in the telescope's field. "Moves pretty quickly, doesn't it?"

Allie looked up from her calculations. "That sucker goes all the way around the world in about an hour and a half."

The roll of film ran out, and Tom rewound it. "Wish I could stay for another run, but it's getting late, and I've got classes tomorrow."

Allie McVeigh looked relieved to kill the view from space. She printed out her calculations and gave a copy to Tom. He tucked it in his pocket and began packing up his gear.

"You'll be back again tomorrow?" Allie asked.

"It depends on how these pictures turn out, and who I talk to," Tom said.

"Well, contact me through the Astronomy Department." She led the way to the exit.

"Thanks a lot, Allie." Tom stopped by the door. "Another favor. Let's keep this whole discovery quiet until we get a line on it."

"Who would I tell?" she said with a lopsided grin as she led the way out. "The scientific world doesn't exactly stop when some little assistant opens her mouth."

Allie went off to her campus housing, and Tom got into his van. As the excitement of his discovery wore off, he yawned all the way home.

Slipping through the doorway of the Swift house, Tom froze as a seven-foot-tall figure rose from the sofa.

"Late night, huh?" The night light glinted off the figure's bright metallic finish.

"Rob, I don't have a curfew. Did Dad leave you to wait up for me?"

The robot went back to the sofa, one of the few pieces of furniture in the house that could support his weight. "Hey, I never sleep. You ought to know that. After all, you invented me."

Tom shook his head. "And where's Orb, your partner in crime?"

Rob couldn't shrug, but he did make an airy gesture with one hand. "He's off thinking deep thoughts. That's what he's built for." Orb and Rob were two units of one machine. Rob was the transit module, and Orb was the computing end.

"Well, Mr. He Who Never Sleeps, here's a job." Tom tossed over the roll of film he'd shot. "Develop this, and have eight-by-tens ready by breakfast." Whistling cheerfully, he went to bed.

The next morning, a yawning Tom stepped into the kitchen to find Rob already waiting for him.

"Your mom and dad were called away early, kid sister Sandra is off on a field trip, and breakfast is waiting." In the breakfast nook, Tom found juice, cereal, milk—and a pile of fresh photos. "What *is* that thing, Tom?"

"It's something about seven hundred miles out in space," Tom began.

"What is?" a new voice butted in as Tom's

11

friend Rick Cantwell bounded into the breakfast nook. "Hey, c'mon. If you can't tell your ride to school, who *can* you tell?"

After seeing the photos and hearing Tom's story, Rick quavered the high-pitched "spooky" music from scary movies: "Ooooh-weee-eeee-oooo!" Then he spoke in a dramatic voice. "You've passed the boundary of everyday reality into an area of mystery, an area of fantasy, an area known as—"

"The Cantwell Zone, I expect," Tom broke in. "Pass those pictures back. I'd like a look before we leave." He stared at them for a long moment, creases appearing on his forehead.

"Are you reading those chicken tracks?" Rick pushed back a lock of sandy hair as he peered over Tom's shoulder.

Tom nodded. "See those squiggles—one, two, three? Looks like they're setting up a number system, but in base fourteen."

"Base fourteen? Instead of base ten?" Rick asked. "What's the deal, Tom? Do guys out there have seven fingers per hand instead of five?"

"I don't know about 'out there,'" Tom responded, "but people here on Earth didn't always count by tens. Some Eskimos worked in base four. The Mayans based their math on the number twenty—do you think they had ten fingers on each hand?"

Rick laughed. "Well, I see that the little

hand on your clock is past the eight, and the big hand is pushing the three. If you don't finish breakfast pretty quick, we'll be late for first period."

Tom got to work on his cereal. After three spoonfuls, the phone rang. Swallowing quickly, Tom picked up the handset. "Swift residence."

"Mr. Swift? This is Dr. de Spain at the computer center. We're having some problems with the programming for the TANC system."

Tom sat up. TANC, the Transformable Ambulatory Nuclear-powered Craft, was Swift Enterprises' hottest project. With its fusion engine and advanced computer-guidance system, this craft could explore deep space. "I'm afraid my father's not in right now. This is Tom junior."

De Spain sounded embarrassed. "Sorry to disturb, then. We're trying to adapt the new guidance system to the space shuttle. Everything gets processed through two computers that actually control the shuttle's flight, plus three backup machines."

"Uh-huh. Five computers run the same data simultaneously but independently," Tom said.

Rick Cantwell tapped him on the shoulder. "We're gonna be real late," he whispered.

"Go on without me," Tom told him. "This may take a while."

13

Rick headed off, sighing. "I know to give up when you start spouting numbers instead of words."

Tom got deeper into the problem, until a movement caught his eye. It was Rob, cleaning the kitchen. A sudden idea hit him. "Dr. de Spain, have you taken up this problem with Orb?"

The man on the other end of the phone was silent for a moment. "Why, no, Tom, I haven't."

Tom grinned in triumph. "I think that's where you'll find your answer—inside Orb. You need simultaneous data processing with constant contact. That's what goes on between Rob and Orb. Check Orb's programming for communication with Rob. Orb may even be able to improve it for you."

The computer expert sounded dubious. "Do you really think. . . ?"

Tom turned to Rob. "Where's Orb right now?"

The big robot paused for a moment, photocell eyes flashing. "Electronics Lab Forty-nine, monitoring some crystal experiments."

"Hear that, Dr. de Spain?" Tom asked.

"I certainly did," the baffled computer man said. "But how did Rob know? Orb was in our lab last night, but he asked a technician for a lift over to Electronics this morning."

Tom knew that Orb would need help moving

from place to place—Rob's computing module was a large silver sphere, with no means of movement. De Spain paused. "Come to think of it, Orb mentioned that Rob wouldn't be available."

"They're in touch, even when separated," Tom explained. "The transponder subroutines might help you with your problem—and Orb is very good at writing machine language."

"It's Orb's native tongue," Rob pointed out.

De Spain chuckled. "Robots that read each other's minds and tell jokes. Where else but at Swift Enterprises?"

They hung up, and Tom looked at the clock. "Where did the time go?" he burst out. "My first class is almost over. If I don't get a move on, I'll be late for second period."

He scooped up the photos and slipped them into a notebook. "I didn't even have a chance to call NASA about these."

Shrugging a book-filled knapsack over one shoulder, he dashed from the house to his van.

On a hillside overlooking the Swift complex—and Tom's home—a figure moved in the dry brush. It was a pale, blond man, short and slim. He wore a camouflage jacket and carried a rifle-shaped object. From his vantage point, he had a perfect view into the

Swift breakfast nook. He waited until Tom had driven onto the road to Central Hills before climbing to the hilltop.

Parked by a narrow dirt road was a sleek, if dusty, sports car. Tossing his high-tech instrument onto the seat, the blond man picked up a cellular phone. Before dialing, he clipped on a security scrambler. The Los Angeles number he punched in was picked up on the second ring.

"Takashima Industries," a pleasant female voice answered. The man smiled, knowing it was generated by a computer. "Ulrich. Code Nine, Zed, Red," he spoke into the receiver.

"Acknowledged," the computer voice said. A high-pitched hum came through the receiver, then the sound of a phone ringing. Again it was picked up on the second ring. This time, Ulrich knew, a person would be on the other end.

"Yes?" The voice on the other end spoke English with a slight hissing accent.

"It's Ulrich, sir. I hope I'm not disturbing you, calling this late. But the program is in motion, and you wanted an immediate report."

"It's barely half past one in the morning here in Tokyo," the voice on the other end said. "I hadn't retired yet. What do you have to report, Ulrich?"

The blond man relaxed a little. "Tom Swift has gone to school, carrying photos from his experiment last night. My compliments to your engineers—the long-range shotgun microphone worked perfectly. Swift's last words before leaving were to regret that he hadn't yet called NASA."

"*Very* good, Ulrich." Even with the slight deadening effect of an international phone line, the voice sounded extremely pleased. "Tom Swift will go to NASA, little knowing that he is setting the stage to destroy both his nation's space program—and Swift Enterprises."

3

TOM SWIFT PULLED INTO THE CENTRAL HILLS High School parking lot. His excuse for lateness—"Swift Enterprises business"—was accepted, and he caught up with his class just as it filed from the classroom.

"You're in luck," Rick Cantwell whispered. "No pop quiz on the Russian Revolution. There's a school assembly instead."

They joined the stream of students heading for the auditorium. Tom found three seats together and sat with Rick to his left and Mandy Coster on his right. Mandy had an envious grin on her pretty face, and her big brown eyes twinkled. "Glad you could join us, Swift," she whispered, tossing her long, chestnut brown hair. "I wish I could claim

18

important business whenever I felt like sleeping a little late."

"Give me a break, Mandy." Tom's cheeks grew warm. "There was a programming problem, and Dad wasn't around. I suggested some subroutines—" He broke off. Why did talking to Mandy always send him off on some boring techno-drone? Dealing with girls was a science he still had to master. "Do we know what the show is today?"

"Let's hope it's not like last month's," Mandy whispered. "Remember 'Our Friend the Clarinet'?"

The head of the science department stepped onto the stage. "Today's visitor comes from the National Aeronautics and Space Administration—NASA, for all you technical illiterates out there. You'll hear about our space effort from a real astronaut, Ms. Sue Chong." The applause was loud, especially from Tom.

"Watch out, Mandy," Rick whispered, leaning across Tom. "I hang pinups of girl rock stars, but Tom's got posters of Sally Ride." Tom gave Rick a dirty look. So he put up pictures of America's first female astronaut. So what?

A young woman in a blue NASA jumpsuit walked onstage. Her dark hair was square-cut, framing a delicate, high-cheekboned face. She smiled at the students as she stepped behind the microphone.

"At the beginning of our space effort, all the astronauts were male military officers with engineering degrees and fifteen hundred hours of flying time as test pilots. Oh yes, they also had to be shorter than five feet eleven to fit into the cramped Mercury space capsules."

She grinned, holding a hand four inches over her head. "Hey, I fit only one of those criteria. I've got a degree in science, have never been a military pilot, and yes, I'm a woman."

Sue Chong leaned forward, her face eager. "Today space has never been more open. You need a thousand hours of piloting jets, twenty-twenty eyesight, and good blood pressure. *Or* you need to have graduated college with highest honors and a degree in science, math, or engineering. You can be as tall as six feet four or as short as five feet. Age isn't a factor. We have one astronaut who's pushing sixty." She picked up a remote control and turned to the projection screen behind her. "Let's see the NASA story—and what your futures can be."

Photos from the sixties appeared as Sue Chong began narrating the story of NASA's space missions, climaxing with the Apollo flights to the Moon. "Then came the next step," she said, flipping to a new set of pictures. "A spacecraft that lifted into orbit and flew down under its own control for a landing. The space shuttle!"

Shuttle triumphs and tragedies followed, trillion-dollar satellite rescues, the *Challenger* disaster, when an entire crew was lost in an explosion. There was even a picture of Sue Chong floating weightless on a recent mission.

"Besides hanging around—literally—I helped test a new low-gravity medical technology. That's the start of a new space business."

A sleek delta-wing form appeared on-screen. "*Moonstalker* is the first of our next generation of space shuttles. Larger, with stronger engines and a computer guidance system developed by Swift Enterprises, this supershuttle will take more people deeper into space."

Beautiful artwork showed the possibilities stemming from the new spacecraft: space stations orbiting Earth, robot mining on the Moon, a lunar colony, expeditions to Mars and to the asteroids. Sue Chong's young listeners responded with shining eyes and lots of applause as she finished.

"Pretty neat, huh, Swift?" Mandy Coster whispered. "Maybe I should become an astronaut."

"From the way Tom's staring at the woman up there, you'd better hurry," Rick joked.

Tom hardly heard. His mind was concentrated on getting Sue Chong to look at the pictures in his knapsack.

When the assembly ended, Tom left his friends. Bucking the tide of exiting students, he headed for the stage. "Ms. Chong!" he called.

The head of the science department noticed Tom and motioned him over. "You mentioned the system under development at Swift Enterprises, Ms. Chong. Well, meet young Tom Swift."

"Great to meet you, Tom," the astronaut said. "When will your father have our guidance system ready? I'm on the shuttle crew for the test flight."

Tom grinned. "It's coming along—I helped out on the programming this morning." He paused for a second. "But I'd like you to see these."

He removed the sheaf of photos from his knapsack. "I was testing an optical-improvement system on a telescope and got this infrared image. It's an object about seven hundred miles up."

Next he showed Allie McVeigh's calculations. "This should help pinpoint its location."

Sue Chong stared warily from the photos to the printout. "Is this some kind of joke?"

"Ms. Chong, I didn't even know you were coming today," Tom said.

The head of the science department shook his head. "Tom isn't given to practical jokes."

Sue Chong placed the photos and printout in her briefcase. "I'm off to the Jet Propulsion Lab in Pasadena. We can look into your data there." She gave Tom a hard look. "If this turns out to be a case of creative photography, you'll live to regret it."

"Whoa!" muttered Tom as the astronaut strode off to reclaim her presentation slides. Rushing off to English lit class for a possible pop quiz on *Moby Dick* was almost a relief.

For the rest of the school day, Tom wrestled with distraction. He'd blown it. Maybe he should have waited for his father to see the pictures and data. Tom Swift, Sr., wouldn't be dismissed as some crazy kid or practical joker.

His bad feelings got worse when he was told to report to the principal's office after classes. Tom didn't even try to think up a comeback when Rick asked, "Somebody in trouble? I wondered who blew up those toilets next door to the chem lab."

Standing at the principal's office was a grim-looking Sue Chong. "All right, Swift. *Something* is up there. People in Pasadena want to talk to you. Now." Tom soon found himself following Sue's official car in his van. Could this be worse than detention? he wondered.

The gate guard at the Jet Propulsion Laboratory passed them through, and Sue drove to a small office building. "In here." She led the way down a hallway to a small, dingy office, where a short, heavyset man stood. "Dr. Trantino, this is Tom Swift."

One look at the man, with his short-sleeved shirt and massed pens in a pocket protector, told Tom that this was a serious engineer.

Sue Chong tapped a thick computer printout on a desk. "Using your coordinates, our tracking radar found an object up there, in a weird, deteriorating orbit. At its apogee, or highest point, the object is seven hundred miles up. Its perigee, when it comes nearest to Earth, is about two hundred twenty-five miles up, brushing the atmosphere. Within four months, the thing will fall to Earth, probably burning away from friction with the air before reaching the ground."

She glanced at Tom. "Whatever is up there, I think it was launched fairly recently—from Earth. And we don't know if the pictures you showed me have any connection with this object."

"Has anyone noticed it before?" Tom asked.

"No. But it *is* in an eccentric orbit," Sue said. "And it won't be around much longer."

She beckoned the scientist forward. "Now, Tom, describe your imaging system to Dr.

Trantino. I don't suppose you know it, but he's an expert in enhanced graphics."

"Are you kidding? My dad has the maps of Ganymede from Voyager One and the last Jupiter probe. Dr. Trantino enhanced the old pictures, as well as the new ones. It was fascinating."

"Ah." Dr. Trantino tried to keep his expression businesslike, but Tom's compliment made his cheeks pink with pleasure. "Now then, if you could describe your apparatus . . ."

Tom explained his new system, and Dr. Trantino nodded. "Yes, that makes sense."

"We'll see how much sense it makes tonight." Sue Chong turned to Tom. "You'll be doing more tests at the San Damian observatory, right?"

When Tom nodded, she said, "Then let's all take a look at what's up there."

In spite of the astronaut's chilly treatment, Dr. Trantino grew progressively warmer as they examined the photos together. "Do you understand the upper part of the inscription?" he asked Tom.

"It provides a set of numerical symbols in base fourteen," Tom said.

The scientist nodded. "And I believe the bottom section gives examples of various math operations." He pointed at one line. "Addition." Then he pointed at another. "Subtraction."

Tom scrutinized the other lines. He pointed to one. "Multiplication?"

"Right!" Dr. Trantino grinned. "And here's division." He shook his head in admiration. "Mathematics is the perfect medium for hypothetical aliens to send messages in. Numbers are more easily decoded than nonhuman language."

Dr. Trantino sent Tom home, but when Tom arrived, his family hadn't returned yet. Dinner was hot dogs à la Rob, while Tom consulted with Orb. Then Tom drove out to the San Damian campus, his equipment in his van. Alison McVeigh was waiting, clearly impressed by Sue Chong and the NASA scientist.

"You mentioned earlier today that whatever's up there must have been recently launched," Tom said to Sue Chong. "Going over the data with a computer, I found another possibility—that the object's in a very old, decaying orbit."

"How old?" Sue Chong asked.

Tom shrugged. "About a million years."

For a second, there was silence. Then Sue Chong spoke curtly to Allie. "Turn the telescope to these coordinates." Turning to Dr. Trantino, she spoke in the same tone. "Please examine this equipment."

Dr. Trantino looked a little embarrassed at this sudden hostility as he disassembled Tom's experimental setup, but he was deft and thorough. "Nothing out of the ordinary," he reported.

"Let's get it set up again," the astronaut said. "With a ninety-minute orbital period, this thing will be passing overhead pretty soon."

With Dr. Trantino's help, Tom had the optical enhancer quickly attached to the telescope.

"There it is." Allie's voice was tight as she pointed to the monitor. The object was still frustratingly blurred.

Tom powered up the laser and cut in his enhancer. The mysterious object jumped into sharper focus.

"What the—?" Tom exclaimed.

The object on the screen was a cube, just as it had been the night before. But instead of the rows of mysterious symbols, there were two round shapes on the upper part of the side facing them, with new lines of symbols below.

Without waiting, Dr. Trantino began operating the infrared camera. "I hope you brought lots of film," he told Tom. "This thing must have writing on more than one side."

For four and a half hours—three orbits—Tom and Dr. Trantino shot pictures of the orbiting object. The strange orbiting cube slowly tumbled through space, revealing different sides of itself—yet only two messages.

Three facets set up the base-fourteen math system. The other message, Tom realized as he stared at the monitor, was a map.

"That's the Moon," Tom said, pointing at the picture of the top circle.

"Exactly!" Dr. Trantino exclaimed excitedly. "The top image is the near side, which we always see from Earth. That second circle is the dark side of the Moon. I worked on a map enhancement program from photos shot by lunar orbiters."

His finger stabbed at a round crater, set in the center of the second image. "But this mark here—the one resembling a spider—doesn't appear in any of our photos."

Sue Chong stared in puzzlement. "What does it mean, then?"

"Unless I miss my guess, the carvings down below are map coordinates," Dr. Trantino said.

"And that spider thing is a sort of 'X marks the spot'?" Tom suggested.

Everyone in the room turned to stare at Tom.

"If it is," Dr. Trantino said in a hushed voice, "that means the 'spot' is in the Hertzsprung Crater on the dark side of the Moon."

Tom gulped. "But who marked it? And what could possibly be hidden there—over a quarter of a million miles away?"

So THE CUBE'S FOR REAL." SUE CHONG'S tight-lipped expression disappeared, to be replaced with a look of wonder. *"Moonstalker* came along at just the right time. We'll be going back to the Moon!"

A blush tinted her delicate features. "Okay, I'm getting a bit carried away. First we'll check out that artifact in orbit." She grinned. *"Then* we'll head for the Moon."

"So tell me," Tom broke in, "does this 'we' include *me?*"

The cheerful atmosphere abruptly evaporated as the NASA employees refused to meet Tom's eyes.

Realization dawned. "Wait a second," Tom said. "Now I understand the little out-of-the-way office, the way you replayed my experiment up here, when NASA has lots of observatories available." He glared. "You're not doing this officially," he said accusingly. "You're doing this whole thing on the sly. I bet nobody else at your lab even knows what I reported."

He began stalking around the observatory. "I didn't even tell my dad what Allie and I found up there. No, I felt it should go straight to NASA. And you guys just jerk me around."

Dr. Trantino had the grace to look upset. "We needed to be sure before we took it further."

"Look, it's my fault," Sue Chong cut in. "*I* had to be sure. If a *Moonstalker* crew member reported a UFO right now, think how the supermarket tabloids would eat it up."

She gestured to Dr. Trantino. "Philip is a friend of mine. He agreed to evaluate your information unofficially. If it turned out to be a hoax . . ." She shrugged. "But it's not, is it? I'm sorry. When I got those photos, I thought you'd been watching too many sci-fi flicks. Instead, you've made one heck of a discovery."

"But is that enough to get me included on the mission of checking it out?" Tom asked.

Sue Chong looked doubtful. "That's not up to Dr. Trantino or to me." She glanced helplessly at Tom. "NASA is a government agency, which means it's a bureaucracy. And the administrator in charge of the next-generation shuttles is—"

"Frederick Napier," Tom finished for her. "Oh, don't be surprised. My dad's developing the guidance system for *Moonstalker*, remember? He deals with the head man."

"Maybe your father can help," Sue suggested.

"Maybe," Tom agreed. "But I wouldn't want to bet. Hey, is that the real time?" He stared at his watch, amazed at how late it had gotten. "Look, I have to get home. Why don't you guys take the film." Tom turned to Allie. "Do you think it will be okay to leave my equipment here?"

She nodded. "Sure. As far as I know, nothing is scheduled here for tomorrow."

"Fine. I'll pick up my stuff either after school or in the evening."

Sue Chong tucked away the rolls of film. "Thanks, Tom." She turned to Allie McVeigh. "Until there's a public announcement . . ."

"I know." Allie's short red curls bobbed as she nodded her head. "Tom already told me."

As Tom pulled into the driveway of the Swift house, he noticed a dim light shining in the living room. Was Rob waiting up for him again? Tom quietly opened the door.

He didn't find the robot sitting on the couch. Instead, Tom's father rose to his feet.

The coffee table was covered with photos—pictures of the strange cube in space. "Rob made me copies from your roll of film," Mr. Swift said. "Mind telling me what's going on?"

Tom ran through the events of the last two days. "I was going to tell you at dinner tonight, but you and Mom weren't home."

"Something came up at our programming facility in San Francisco. One of our top people just quit, leaving big holes in a lot of projects." Mr. Swift gave his son a wry smile. "By the way, nice catch on that TANC glitch. Your suggestion has us up and running, which will make tomorrow afternoon's meeting a lot easier."

"You're seeing someone from NASA tomorrow?"

Tom's father nodded. "Frederick Napier—the head of the *Moonstalker* project."

Tom grinned. "When you talk with him, there's something I'd like to ask for. . . ."

The next afternoon, Tom headed for his van the moment classes ended. He took the quickest shortcuts to Swift Enterprises, eager to get there as soon as possible. Napier's meeting with Tom's father was supposed to go on for some time, but what if the NASA official left early?

As Tom burst into the administration building, Mary Ann Jennings looked up from the reception desk. "Cool your jets, Tom. He's still here."

Tom skidded on his way to the elevators. How did that woman know everything going on at Swift Enterprises?

When he arrived at the top floor of the building, Tom headed down a thickly carpeted hallway. His father's administrative assistant passed him straight in.

Afternoon sunlight slanted in through the windows, glinting off models representing three generations of inventions. Judging from the stern expression of the gray-haired man sitting in front of his father's desk, these past glories didn't cut much ice with Frederick Napier. The heavy-boned NASA administrator seemed a little too large, and warm, for the navy blue suit he was wearing. A small roll of fat bulged over the top of his white shirt collar. It was all the more noticeable thanks to his close-cropped haircut.

Napier turned a red face as Tom stepped in. "So this is the great discoverer himself, eh?"

A muscle quirked in Tom senior's cheek, but he remained polite. "This is my son, Tom."

"Let's get to it," the NASA man said bluntly. "I came here today to see if we can push up the testing on the TANC guidance system for

Moonstalker. And what do you start talking about? Arranging a NASA junket for your kid. That sounds like a holdup to me, and I don't like it."

Tom could see why his father was having such a job controlling his temper.

"Mr. Napier, I promised all my support to meet your new schedule," Mr. Swift said stiffly. "Then I merely raised the possibility—"

"Of letting the discoverer of that erratically orbiting object take part in the mission to examine it," Tom put in. "Mr. Napier, I freely admit that Alison McVeigh and I stumbled across that artifact by accident. But my new imaging system did produce legible photos of the inscriptions. I even helped on the programming to enable *Moonstalker*'s control computers to work in tandem. Doesn't that earn me something?"

Napier's face only got redder. "Son, let me explain something. NASA is supported by taxpayer money. That means Congress approves our budget, which means a lot of politics. It also means we have to be able to point to solid successes."

He scowled. "That's been difficult in recent years. It took us a long time to get over losing one of our shuttles. And when we got the *Challenger* disaster behind us, there was the problem with the space telescope. NASA has had enough technical black eyes. I want the *Moonstalker* launch to be a complete success."

Napier glared at both Swifts. "Now you ask me to jeopardize this mission by taking along an untrained crew member. Even worse, one who just happens to be the son of a contractor helping to build the new shuttle."

He shook his head. "And what is this mission supposed to be doing? Looking for little green men. Do you two get it? We have a tough enough job without a lot of stupid publicity."

Mr. Swift turned to his son. "Mr. Napier has discussed the situation with the top levels of NASA. They want to put off any announcement about the artifact until after the super-shuttle has gone up to examine it." He glanced at the NASA man. "I've already agreed to maintain silence from the Swift Enterprises end of the operation."

Tom nodded. "That makes sense. I suppose Sue Chong told you I'd already asked Allie McVeigh, the assistant at the San Damian observatory, to do the same thing."

Napier relaxed a little. "I appreciate your help. The space program doesn't need to be turned into a cheap media circus."

Just then, the speakerphone on Mr. Swift's desk rang. Tom senior punched a button, and a harassed-sounding voice rang through the room.

"Mr. Swift?" Tom immediately recognized the slightly raspy tones of Harlan Ames, the head of Swift security. He was nearly drowned out by crowd noises in the background. "We've got a bit of a situation at the main gate."

"I'll be down to see Mr. Napier off," Mr. Swift said quickly. "Then I'll join you." He punched off the phone and rose from his chair. "Mr. Napier, rest assured we'll speed up our development of TANC technology. All I ask is that you consider my son's proposal."

Napier seemed to thaw a little on the way down in the elevator. He even paused for a moment to admire the older Swift rocket engines mounted for display on the lobby walls.

"Now, NASA *will* announce Tom's discovery and give him full credit. We just want a chance to examine the artifact first. As for the rest of your request—" Napier took a deep breath as they left the building. "Well, I'll inquire—"

The rest of his words were cut off by a roar from the main entrance as a crowd surged against the gates. Tom, his father, and Frederick Napier froze in their tracks. Several people in the surging group were aiming TV minicams at them. Tom recognized the logos of all the major networks.

"Reporters!" Napier said in disgust. "What do they want?"

Even over the uproar, they could hear some of the questions being bawled at them.

"Is it true that Tom Swift has discovered a message from space aliens orbiting above us?" a leather-lunged reporter shouted.

"Is answering this message the mission of the *Moonstalker*?" another newscaster called out.

Another reporter yelled too, her voice almost a shriek. "Will Tom Swift be aboard?"

5

FREDERICK NAPIER'S FACE WENT EVEN REDDER than the tie he was wearing. "What's the idea, Swift?" he growled, turning on Tom's father. "You told me upstairs that your people would keep quiet about this whole alien artifact situation. Then the moment I step out of your offices, I find jackasses from all the networks and most of the cable companies, asking dumb questions."

He gave Tom an especially angry glare. "Don't think I missed that most of the questions were about you, boy genius. I hate grandstand plays, especially when they're designed to force my hand. And I speak for NASA." Napier stormed off to his car, ignoring the shouted questions from the gate.

Tom and his father watched as the car's engine started. Napier lowered his window. "Is there some other way out of here—one that won't take me past those bozos?"

Sighing, Mr. Swift beckoned Harlan Ames away from the crowd. The head security man's tanned, leathery face was pink with embarrassment. "Mr. Swift, I'm sorry."

"Can't be helped, Harlan," Tom's father said. "Take Mr. Napier to the north gate. And get a public relations person over to that crowd. Whatever the question, our answer is 'No comment.'"

As Tom followed his father back to his office, Mr. Swift didn't say a word. But Tom felt unasked questions thick between them.

Tom Swift, Sr., strode over to punch a button on a desktop console. One wall suddenly turned into a holograph. The image on the screen, however, was the late afternoon cable news.

One look told the Swifts how the media had gotten wind of Tom's discovery. A reporter stood in the San Damian observatory, pointing at Tom's equipment, still hooked up to the telescope. "The two graduate students, coming in for an early morning observation, found the Swift Enterprises apparatus. Testing it yielded these photographs."

The screen now filled with slightly blurry

but still recognizable images. The unearthly script was clear enough.

Tom gulped. "I was going to pick that stuff up a little later."

Now the reporter was in close-up.

"Consulting the log of telescope users, we found the name of Tom Swift, the young inventor who developed the Swift portable satellite dish and the Z-27 aeronautic fuel. A USC-San Damian teaching assistant, Alison McVeigh, was also logged in, but we haven't been able to find her for a comment yet."

A buzz came from the speakerphone on the desk. "Mr. Swift, Dan Smathers is on your personal phone line, asking for an interview."

Tom gaped. "Dan Smathers? The lead newscaster on the seven o'clock national news? How did he get your private number?"

Tom's father looked grim. "That's what I'd like to know." He punched a button and told his office assistant, "Thank Mr. Smathers, but tell him I have no comment right now."

He turned. "Welcome to the big time, Tom. You're about to become a media star for a while."

Luckily, the Swift house was inside the perimeter fence of Swift Enterprises. Tom and his father were able to drive home without getting swamped by overeager media people. Walking through the door, Tom found his mother shaking her head. "Dear," she said to

Tom senior, "Ted Rokaw called here asking for an interview with you."

Tom's sister, Sandra, grinned at him. "I heard your name all over the TV, too."

"Great." Tom rolled his eyes.

"Oh, and some girl called, too, before we started screening everything with the answering machine," Sandra continued. "Her name's Allie. So what's the story, Tom? Is she a science groupie?"

Tom glanced at his parents. "That must have been Alison McVeigh, the astronomy assistant who helped me discover the cube," he said. "So far, she hasn't given any media interviews. Looks like she's keeping the promise of secrecy she made."

"She said she'd call again," Sandra added.

"If she wants help keeping that promise, tell Alison she can come here," Mr. Swift said. "Harlan Ames will figure a way to get her in."

While waiting for Allie to call back, Tom answered a call on the internal line to the administration building. It was Harlan Ames. "Tell your father we had our first visitor from the lunatic fringe. Some guy tried to smuggle himself in by hiding in a packing case. Calls himself the president of a group called the IFA—Interplanetary Friends of Aliens."

Tom had to hold back a laugh. "Well, now we have a way to smuggle Allie McVeigh in."

He passed the handset to his father so he could explain the situation to Harlan.

Just then the outside phone began ringing. The answering machine picked up. "I'm leaving a message for Tom Swift," a nervous voice said. "This is Alison McVeigh—"

Tom cut in. "Allie! Where are you? What happened to you?"

"Right now I'm in a diner off-campus in San Damian, after coming back to my dorm and finding nine million reporters hanging around. A friend told me about the news leaking out, but so far NASA hasn't said anything. So I decided to stay away. They've run my picture on TV, trying to find me." She giggled. "They got hold of my student ID photo, which looks nothing like me."

"My dad says that if you have no place to go, we'll put you up," Tom offered.

Allie gave a sigh of relief. "I was hoping for some help."

Tom grinned. "Give me the address of the diner, and I'll send somebody to get you."

The next morning, the Swift family and Allie McVeigh sat in the living room, watching the continuing media storm. They saw a reporter standing guard at the main gate to Swift Enterprises, doing a little happy talk with the anchorpeople on the morning wakeup show.

"Harlan tells me there are camera crews at all our exits," Mr. Swift said. "Unless you intend to fly out this morning—"

The scene on the TV changed to show a reporter staking out the front of Central Hills High. Tom rolled his eyes. "Looks like I'll be missing classes today."

Next came a reporter at the San Damian campus. Allie sighed. "That makes two of us."

Kathy Kerrick, the female anchor, suddenly cut in with the announcement of a special news conference in Washington.

The scene changed yet again, to show the NASA seal and Frederick Napier at a lectern. The administrator's face was bright red as he spoke.

"The discovery by Tom Swift and Alison McVeigh poses a great mystery to the people of Earth—a mystery we at NASA intend to investigate. This investigation will be the first mission of the newest addition to our shuttle fleet, *Moonstalker.* I have been assured that the supershuttle will be ready for flight in one month's time."

Napier cleared his throat, and his face turned almost purple. "One of the major public responses has been the question of whether the crew for any investigation will include Tom Swift, Jr. I am happy to announce—"

"He doesn't look too happy," Sandra said.

"—that NASA is inviting both discoverers, Mr. Swift and Ms. McVeigh, to participate in the *Moonstalker* mission. Their participation may even extend to performing as mission specialists on the flight itself."

Tom and Allie turned to stare at each other. "All *right!*" Tom burst out.

"The only factors restricting this invitation are health and safety considerations," Napier went on. "The candidates must meet the necessary medical requirements and must complete astronaut training before the mission date."

"I knew there had to be a catch," Allie groused. "The last time they took a complete civilian on a shuttle, it took four months to train her."

Napier made some closing remarks, but Tom was no longer listening. He turned to Allie. "Does that mean you aren't going to give it a try?"

"And miss a chance to work at NASA?" Allie shook her head vigorously, and her red curls flew around her face. "Of course I'm going to try! What about you?"

Tom grinned. "Do you even have to ask?"

As they shook hands, laughing, the internal phone rang. Mr. Swift answered, then turned to Tom. "It's NASA, with your official invitation. By the way, you're expected at Edwards Air Force Base in an hour for your physical exam."

*   *   *

In a Century City hotel suite, a short, slim man switched off the television. Dressed in a black silk suit, Ulrich looked far different from the camouflaged spy who had eavesdropped on the Swift household. He slipped a scrambler over the hotel telephone and dialed a local number. Right after the second ring, the phone was picked up—with a mechanical click.

"Takashima Industries," the pleasant, female-sounding computer voice said.

"Ulrich," the blond man said. "Code Nine, Zed, Red."

He wondered if the code words were even necessary. A high-tech company like the one Yuri Takashima had put together might have a voiceprint analyzer hitched to the phone. All the machine needed was a few words to match his voiceprint to a file in the Takashima computers. The only answer he got was the computer's "Acknowledged."

The high-pitched hum followed, then the sound of another phone ringing. It was picked up after two rings. Ulrich wondered how the boss always managed to do that.

"Yes?" the slightly accented voice on the other end said.

"It's Ulrich, sir. Everything continues to go as planned. The leaked information has created a media fire storm."

"This leak cannot be traced?" the voice hissed.

"The pair of college kids who spread the news don't even know they're being used," Ulrich explained. "They had a legitimate reason to use the observatory. All I had to do was arrange a scheduling change to send them there while Swift's equipment was still connected."

"Excellent," the faraway voice said. "And has this media attention had the desired result?"

"The American space program has just given in," Ulrich said. "Tom Swift, Jr., has even been offered a place on the new supershuttle."

"Splendid work, Ulrich," the man on the phone said. "As I, of course, expected."

The man hung up, staring out the window of his penthouse, taking in the nighttime view of Tokyo spread out below. Smiling, he turned to the servant moving silently behind him. "You see, Ishi, Europeans are especially good at certain tasks, while the people of Asia excel at others. As a citizen of the world, I can pick and choose, using both to the best advantage. Thus I have made the world my own."

The smile turned colder. "And soon, after the Americans—especially Swift—have been dealt with, I will make *all* the worlds my own."

6

TOM SWIFT'S PHYSICAL EXAMINATION WAS just the beginning. And as Tom was to learn, the physical was the *easy* part. The next three weeks flew by quickly in a rush of hard work and preparation. Some things stood out in Tom's memory, though.

His initial training took place at Edwards Air Force Base, where the space shuttles landed. After arranging a leave of absence from school, Tom discovered that he faced a hundred and twenty hours of classes.

"You're expected to know everything there is in this." A hostile NASA staffer handed Tom and Allie each an inches-thick binder. "This manual tells you how the shuttle works, system by system. It tells you what buttons to push and which never to touch. When we've finished testing you on it, you'll know everything from how to get into the shuttle to how to use the toilets."

"Toilets?" Tom echoed.

The NASA man shrugged. "How many toilets have you seen that need a seat belt and foot restraints?"

Shaking his head, Tom turned to Allie. "I don't think we're in Kansas anymore," he said.

Allie stared at the thick binder as if she feared there was a bomb inside. "If they expect me to swallow everything in this and spit it back in quizzes, I don't think I'll be on that shuttle."

"Come on, Allie," Tom tried to console her. "Our training can't be all classes."

He was right about that. The doctors took seven vials of blood, asked six hundred and sixty-eight questions about their health, and spent three hours poking and prodding them, followed by strength tests. Then the dirty tricks began.

Tom waited outside a room as Allie went in. Moments later a wild scream rang out. Tom dashed to the doorway and froze, staring. Allie seemed to be hooked up to a dentist's chair, but this was worse than going to the dentist. The chair spun like a top!

"We're testing how disoriented she'll get

in a weightless environment," a technician explained.

"I can hardly wait for my turn," Tom muttered.

He felt even more disoriented that evening, watching TV in the visitors' video lounge. The newspeople couldn't get in to question him, but "Tom-mania," as it was now called, raged on. Tom couldn't believe how far the news hounds were willing to go to get a story. There was a reporter on the steps of Central Hills High, interviewing a blushing Mandy Coster!

"So, Mandy," the reporter said, shoving a microphone at her. "Tell us a little bit about life with Tom Swift. I bet there are a lot of girls who'd like to be in your shoes."

"In my—? What are you talking about?" Mandy asked.

"Well, everyone knows that you're Tom Swift's girlfriend," the reporter replied.

"G-girlfriend?" Mandy repeated.

Tom rolled his eyes. Great, he thought. It's a toss-up who'll win the award for the world's reddest face, Mandy Coster or Frederick Napier. He got up and left the lounge in disgust.

Footsteps sounded behind him, and Tom turned to see Allie McVeigh. "Is she really your girlfriend?" she asked.

"She might have considered it, once," Tom

said, shaking his head. "After this, I don't think so."

Allie gave him a grin. "I think they call it the price of fame."

"Yeah." Tom looked down. "But it's all nonsense! 'Tom-mania.'" He snorted. "I'm a nationwide hero, but I haven't done one thing to deserve it."

"Like being a rock star when you're only lip-synching?" Allie shook her head. "Is that why you won't give press interviews? The NASA public relations people were expecting you to."

"I can't believe those guys want us to waste time talking to reporters when we have only a month to learn so much stuff."

Allie nodded and rubbed her eyes. "Speaking of which, I'm going back to crack the books. Which is the cabin fan control and which adjusts the cabin temperature?"

Tom watched Allie leave with concern in his eyes. She was confused by the air and water controls? He'd soaked up that section in his first night's reading. "Maybe she *won't* be on the supershuttle," he muttered.

But as the days went on and Allie struggled more and more with the book learning, she strove to match Tom's success. A week or so into training, she drew Tom aside as they headed out of classes. "Don't let anybody talk you into spicy Mexican food for dinner. I heard some guys talking about taking us for a flight in the KC-One-Thirty-Five. You know what *that* means."

Tom nodded. "Weightless training."

The pilot on the testing plane next morning was a lot friendlier than most of the NASA people they had dealt with. "Strapped in back there?" he asked as they taxied down the runway.

"We're fine," Tom said.

"You won't be soon," the pilot cheerfully replied. As soon as they were in the air, he continued in a steep ascent. Then, six miles high, he whipped the craft around, plunging them earthward.

Allie's curls suddenly went floating up from her head. The chain she was wearing tried to lift off her neck. "YOW!" she cried.

Following procedure, Tom unstrapped himself and sailed out of his seat. Allie followed, soaring over Tom's shoulders in an impromptu game of leapfrog—while Tom was still in midair!

"Weird," Tom said as the impact of Allie's hands on his shoulders sent him drifting to the floor in slow motion. He bounced off and floated away. It was like swimming but without water.

For the next two hours, the pilot put the plane through loop-the-loops while Tom and

Allie played and worked. They tossed balls, then tested their coordination by tying knots and slipping into spacesuits.

After the twentieth dive, Tom began to hear ominous gurglings deep in his stomach. He tried swallowing, but that didn't help much. Glancing at Allie, he saw her face had gone a pale green.

"Know what they call this plane?" the pilot asked cheerfully.

"What?" Allie croaked.

"The vomit comet," the pilot replied. "Don't feel bad if you think you're going to lose it. We've had United States senators blow lunch aboard this baby."

Lurching around the plane's cabin, Allie grabbed her airsickness bag. When they finally landed, Tom caught Allie as she dropped from the plane's hatch. "Some people will give everything for the cause," he said, smiling.

"Including breakfast," she groaned.

"Cheer up. We'll be going for lunch soon."

Allie shut her eyes tight. "Oh, I can hardly wait."

The weeks of training went on. Despite the heavy load, Tom kept up, and Allie tried gamely. Slowly the NASA people warmed to them, admiring their efforts. By the end of three weeks, technicians and teachers were cheering them on.

At the end of their ordeal, Tom and Allie were invited to the head trainer's office.

"We're sorry," the head trainer said to Allie. From his tone of voice, Tom thought, the man really meant it. "You still haven't shown that you know enough about the shuttle's systems. I've already spoken with Houston, however, and you'll be one of the Ground Control crew. I'm sure the PR people will like that."

"Getting some use out of me, you mean," Allie said, then sighed. "Well, I guess that's the closest I'll come."

"Look at it this way—you'll be on national television." Smiling, the head trainer turned to Tom. "Congratulations. You've passed the tests. They're expecting you at Cape Canaveral to join the shuttle crew for final training."

"When do I leave for Florida?" Tom asked.

"Tomorrow morning."

"I'll have to make a few phone calls—final preparations, you might say."

One call brought a Swift Enterprises helicopter to the base, to take him back to Central Hills. Another call was to Mandy Coster.

They met that evening on the beach at Laguna Pequeña. "We've walked along this stretch of sand before," Mandy said, staring at the moonlight rippling on the waves. "It was our first—"

Tom smiled. "Date, sort of?"

Mandy nestled closer to him. "I guess." She gazed at the cloudless sky above. "I remember we had a moon that night, too." She laughed, but it wasn't a happy sound. "Who would have guessed back then that you'd be going up there in person?"

"Not me," Tom admitted. "Look, I've been really busy with this training stuff. Maybe I should have called, but—well, I didn't know if you would talk to me, after that stupid TV interview." He looked down. "Anyway, I asked Dad to make the guest arrangements for the launch. Rick will be going to Florida."

Now he looked up. "But you said no."

Mandy shook her head. "I—I don't think I could." She gulped. "What if it turned out like the *Challenger?*"

The mention of the space shuttle that had blown up at launching sent Mandy into Tom's arms.

"I couldn't stand it, Tom," she whispered into his chest. "Let me stay home to watch on TV."

They looked into each other's eyes for a moment. Then Mandy kissed him. "Good luck, Tom," she whispered. "Come home safe."

Tom Swift sat in the rear of the flight deck, his shoulders tight under their straps. "T minus ten," a voice came over the loudspeaker. As the seconds ticked off, Tom glanced around at the other figures in their acceleration seats. At the controls was Captain Chuck Nelson, an astronaut of the old school. He was short, his thinning hair was shaved to a brush cut, and his erect, military bearing screamed "air force."

Beside Nelson at the control console was Neal Tyrone. The husky young man towered over the mission commander. They looked like a football star and his coach, but they worked together like a well-trained team as they went down the pre-lift-off flight checks.

To Tom's left was Sue Chong, her fine features tensed as if she could will the countdown to go faster. Off to the side and behind him were the two scientists on the mission, another pair of contrasts. Professor Alvin Packard was plump, pink-skinned, and cheerful, while Professor Fedor Domovoy was tall, stooped, and gloomy-looking. Tom pulled his thoughts back on track as the countdown reached zero and ignition hit.

A jolt struck the flight deck. Out the side windows, Tom saw the ground and launch tower disappearing behind them. The sky got darker. They were up, almost out of the atmosphere . . .

Another jolt hit them, this time an unexpected one. Alarms began screaming.

"Losing fuel!" Chuck Nelson yelled. "We're not going to make it."

Neal Tyrone, the copilot, began hitting keys, his dark face taut as he scanned the information running across his computer screen. "We're too high to land on the emergency fields in Spain and Africa."

Nelson was also working on the control console. "We'll establish a low orbit to bring us once around, then land."

They felt a lesser jolt as the maneuvering rockets cut in. A sigh rose from the rest of the crew. "Okay. We're in a safe orbit," Nelson reported.

Then a voice came over the loudspeaker. "Good work, people. Excellent dress rehearsal. You can leave the simulator now."

"Why don't *you* open the hatch, Tom?" Sue Chong said.

"Checking to make sure I can do it?" Tom asked as he swung the heavy door open.

"Let's get some rest," Captain Nelson said. "We'll be up early for tomorrow's launch."

Early wasn't the word for it. *Moonstalker* was scheduled for a dawn launch, so Tom and the other crew members were up well before sunrise. They rode out to the fixed service structure, a tower that loomed beside their spacecraft, in the predawn dimness. The craft itself gleamed in the brilliant arc lights surrounding the launch pad.

Tom knew the huge rocket boosters would soon be obsolete when the Swift fusion engines were fitted to the spacecraft. For now, though, the huge engines were the last word in power, turning the craft into a giant white arrow pointed at the heavens. And the arrow's tip was *Moonstalker*.

Tom knew that the stubby-winged supershuttle was big. But at the top of a skyscraper-tall rocket, it seemed small and vulnerable. Pushing the word *Challenger* out of his head, Tom boarded the elevator that would take him to the orbiter access arm.

Two hours later, Tom's muscles ached from tension as he sat strapped into his launch seat. At least, no problems big enough to halt the countdown had arisen. They reached the ten-second mark. Beside him, Tom heard Sue Chong suck in a deep breath as the mission controller's voice counted down their final seconds. "Two, one . . . Ignition!"

Again, a jolt hit the flight deck, but this time it was for real. Funny, Tom thought. He'd been on roller coaster rides worse than this. He thought of other launches he had seen. How absurdly slowly the spaceships had seemed to move, balancing precariously on their tails of flame.

He tried not to count off the passing time.

The *Challenger* had exploded seventy-two seconds after lift off. Surely they were past that by now!

In front of a television set in Tokyo, a man sat watching the launch. "*Moonstalker* is now in orbit," the announcer said. "The first stage of the mission is completed."

The man touched a remote control, and the ascending shuttle disappeared. "Not the first stage." His thin lips stretched in a cruel smile. "It's the third stage of my plan to wreck the Swifts—and seize control of space for myself."

7

ABOARD THE SPACE SHUTTLE, CAPTAIN CHUCK
Nelson communicated with ground control.
"Control, this is *Moonstalker*. OMS-two burn
commencing."

Tom knew that Nelson was about to ignite
the Orbital Maneuvering System engines for
the second time, guiding them into orbit a
hundred and twenty miles above the Earth.

He felt a surge as the rockets kicked in.
Then they stopped. "OMS-two cutoff," Nelson
reported. "We're in orbit."

"Roger, *Moonstalker*. Control out." Nelson
flicked a switch on the automatic pilot. "Well,
crew, we're officially up. For those of you
who've never been here before, welcome to
space."

59

He reached over to shake hands with his copilot, Neal Tyrone, who grinned. Tom knew it was Tyrone's first shuttle flight. Nelson had served as copilot on other missions. The only other "old space hand" aboard was Sue Chong.

"Look alive, Swift," she called from the seat next to him. "I'm trying to shake with you." As he reached over, Tom felt the eerie sensation of weightlessness. His hand missed Sue's, but she caught it, grinning. "You'll get used to this pretty quickly."

"I hope so," Tom muttered. He exchanged waves with Domovoy and Packard, the scientists chosen to go up and examine the strange artifact above the Earth. The gloomy Domovoy was a language expert, while the cheerful Packard, a geologist, was there to determine what the mysterious cube was made of.

"I'm opening the doors of the cargo bay," Nelson announced. Standard procedure, Tom knew. The doors helped radiate heat away from the shuttle.

Nelson unstrapped himself. "We'll be making a course correction to swing into that cube's orbit. Before we do so, I want everyone to check their action stations."

He turned to Tom. "You take a look at the Swift equipment." He paused. "Especially our extra—uh, passengers—downstairs."

Tom nodded and undid his shoulder harness. Even that small motion set him floating out of his seat. Before he got stranded in mid-air, Tom extended a foot and pushed. He soared off like a toy balloon on a gust of wind, floating over Sue Chong's head.

Moving in microgravity wasn't exactly like flying, Tom decided. It was more like making a tricky bank shot on a pool table. Except *he* was the billiard ball, and the "pocket" he'd aimed for was the hatchway leading to the level below the flight deck.

Tom rose to the ceiling, took most of the shock with his hands, and pushed off gently. His new course took him right through the open hatch. Sue Chong grinned at him. "You're getting the hang of things already."

Tom floated through the opening. It was a weird feeling, having to *pull* himself down the rungs of a ladder. The middeck was about the size of his living room back home, twenty by thirty feet. But this was the only "living space" for a good seven hundred miles around. Six people would cook, eat, sleep, and hang out here. The seventh and eighth crew members had lifted off strapped to the rear wall of the middeck, their backs to an unyielding metal wall. An uncomfortable launch for humans—but then, they weren't humans.

"Hey, boss," Rob greeted Tom. "Can I untie us now?"

"I should like to experience weightless floating," Orb added.

"Do that," Tom said. "I want to test Rob's programming for weightless walking." One of the toughest jobs in building Rob had been designing him to walk on two legs. Tom was eager to see how his creation handled micro-gravity—the near-weightlessness of space.

Rob undid his restraints, tried to rise—and flung himself all over the room. Tom dodged, keeping to the ceiling as the robot clanged about. "What's going on down there?" a call came from the flight deck.

"My robot is getting used to low gravity," Tom replied. "Rob, use the open parameters I left in the programming to adjust your reactions."

"Right." After a few false starts, Rob was soon floating elegantly, softly bouncing from wall to wall.

A buzzer went off. "We're coming up on the object," Captain Nelson warned. "Everyone strap in for final course corrections."

Rob bounded for his straps as Tom hauled himself up the ladder. Moments later, he was in his seat. While he'd been downstairs, Sue Chong had slipped on her microgravity shoe attachments. The metal footplates with suction cups on the bottom looked like something out of a cartoon. But they'd hold her in place at the aft crew station while she worked the remote manipulator arm to snag the object in space.

Tom knew that on a previous mission Sue had already deployed a multiton communications satellite using the double-jointed crane arm. But catching a small orbiting body that lacked standard handles would be different. Still, Sue looked confident as the reaction control rockets brought them around slightly.

"Okay." Neal Tyrone rose from his control console, and he and Sue carefully floated to the rear station and planted their feet, attaching themselves to the deck. Tyrone would handle last-minute course corrections while Sue operated the crane. Her control was a big joystick, like something from a video game. She even had a screen in front of her, showing the view from a video camera at the end of the mobile arm.

"Here it comes," Neal Tyrone warned. Sue gripped the joystick.

This would not be an easy job, Tom knew. NASA engineers had developed a new grappler—a net that pulled tight on command.

Her face tense, Sue shifted the joystick around. Tom could imagine her in a video game room, killing thousands of alien spaceships. But could she catch the strange cube?

Suddenly Sue pulled the trigger on the joystick. "Snagged it!" she cried triumphantly.

The two professors were out of their seats, eager for their first close-up look at the mysterious artifact.

"Give me a break, guys," Sue told them. "Let me reel this sucker in."

She was still working the joystick, bringing the arm and its burden back into the open cargo bay.

The two scientists crowded around her video screen. First Packard asked for a camera close-up of the cube, his round cheeks pink with excitement.

"Just as we thought from the albedo—the light reflected off the object," he said. Tom smiled at the techno-talk. "It's made of stone—solid, apparently, since I don't see any joints or cracks in it."

"What sort of stone?" Domovoy asked, his deep voice heavily accented.

"Igneous rock—stone that was once molten lava. I'd say it was like granite." Packard squinted at the screen. "The outside of the cube was vitrified, that is, exposed to tremendous heat until it became glassy."

"Then came someone—or something, I suppose, to cut those symbols into it." Domovoy's long face was the liveliest Tom had seen it as he peered intently at the carved math lesson. "Maybe done by a laser-type device."

Tom joined the crowd at the rear of the cabin, but there was no way he could get close to the screens. He contented himself by looking out the rear windows. Then he froze.

"The cube was relatively easy to spot, once

we knew where to look because of its ability to reflect light. Or as you would say, it had a high albedo. Right?" Tom asked.

"Correct," Packard replied.

"Well, something else out there is blotting out some stars. We probably wouldn't have noticed it from Earth. Here it shows up more clearly. And it doesn't seem to have *any* albedo."

In spite of his excitement over the alien cube, Captain Nelson turned from the screen and joined Tom. "A black body—that's the military term for it," Nelson said, peering out. "That's perfect camouflage in the darkness of space." He beckoned Tyrone over. "Check this out."

Domovoy and Packard stayed glued to the screen, studying the alien cube, while the others turned to stare at this unexpected object.

After some radar and computer work, they'd established that the new mystery body was following the same orbit as the cube.

"It could be that whoever left the first object up here left something to keep an eye on it," Tom finally said. "I think we should take a closer look."

"No way we can do that on this orbit," Sue objected. "We'd have to get that cube out of the net and reset the remote arm."

Tom shook his head. "That's not what I meant. If this second object was designed as a black body to escape detection, I don't think we should take this ship anywhere near it."

Captain Nelson frowned in thought. "You're thinking of an EVA?"

Nelson meant an Extra-Vehicular Activity, a trip outside the spacecraft. "Exactly," Tom said.

"Using that new, Swift-designed Manned Maneuvering Unit?" Sue asked.

Tom shrugged. "Well, I'm the one who helped design the mini-MMU. And the test unit fits only my suit."

He looked for a long moment at Sue. The crew had been friendly after he'd survived astronaut testing, but this was the crunch. Either he'd get to work on this mission, or he might as well sack out in one of the sleeping compartments. "Hey," he pointed out, "I *am* the most expendable."

"Sure," Sue muttered. "It would be no great loss if we let the boy astronaut croak."

The protest came, surprisingly, from the professors. Packard's chubby face went bright red. "*We're* supposed to be going out there!" he said.

"He's right!" Even Domovoy's face showed color. "Capturing the cube and studying it *is* our mission, after all. That other object will still be there after we finish."

Nelson frowned. "Why can't we do both?" he asked. "We're orbiting close enough to this mystery object to give you a chance, Swift. Suit up first and get over to that thing. Sue, help him. Professors, after Tom has gone through the airlock, you'll have your EVA."

Tom went down to the middeck, into the privacy compartment. When he emerged, he wore a spandex bodysuit with tubes attached for circulating air and coolant.

Tom stepped into the airlock, and Sue handed him the suit bottom, which resembled a pair of baggy pants. At the same time, Sue let the suit top float above Tom's head. Coming up from a deep knee bend, Tom slipped into the top. Sue connected electrical circuits and the air and liquid hoses, and then Tom sealed the suit up.

"You're sure you want to do this?" she asked.

"Let's just get the harness connected," Tom said. The Swift jet pack was smaller and much less bulky than the standard MMUs aboard. Instead of surrounding Tom like the back of a big armchair, his jets fit in a compact package at the small of his back. A pair of control arms jutted out at elbow height. Resting his forearms on these, Tom could comfortably fit his fingers on the control surfaces. Tom checked the electrical circuits and his air flow, and drew on a pair of heavy gauntlets. "Ready to roll." He put on his helmet. Rob closed the airlock's inner door.

"Testing." Tom spoke into his suit radio's mike.

"You're coming in fine," Nelson's voice crackled on Tom's headset. "Get going, Tom. The professors are champing at the bit."

Tom hit the first switch on the airlock's wall control panel, and pumps began sucking air from the tiny room. Soon the atmosphere was a mere five pounds per square inch, as thin as at the top of Mount Everest. Tom's suit began to balloon out. He hit a second switch. In three minutes, vacuum surrounded him. The outer door opened, and Tom was in space.

Tom stepped into the open cargo bay, staring at the stars above. He was amazed at how sharp the stars were. They seemed to float just out of reach, beyond his helmet bubble. Tom sighted on the small dot of the mystery satellite and triggered his rockets. The shuttle seemed to sink below him as he angled upward. "You're right on course," Nelson said over the radio.

The dark object grew larger, blotting out more stars. Tom could make it out as a black sphere. Was that the glint of a lens?

Tom would never know. At that moment, the object disappeared in a brilliant orange flash.

*   *   *

Halfway around the world, in a high-tech command post, a young man stared at a computer screen, then got on the telephone. His call was answered on the second ring. "Yes?"

"Sir," the young technician said. "A message came in through our covert orbital network. The watcher satellite at prime location has ceased even passive information-gathering and gone into explosive shutdown mode."

There was a hiss of indrawn breath. "Ah," said the man on the other end. "I had hoped to get more information on this new super-shuttle in action, but my surveillance satellite must have been noticed. Its programming initiated the self-destruct sequence."

His laugh was chilling. "I hope we didn't scald any curious cats."

8

IT TOOK TOM A SECOND TO REALIZE HE'D JUST seen an explosion in the soundlessness of space.

"Tom! Get out of there—fast!" Captain Nelson's voice burst from Tom's earphones. "You're going to get hit by the shock wave from that blast and the flying debris!"

Tom's hands went to the jet controls. Nothing to worry about, he told himself. The body of his spacesuit was made of metal mesh alloy, and the material in the pants and arms could stop bullets. Still . . .

He began to turn back toward the ship. Just as his suit's jets fired, the blast wave hit him. He was sent tumbling, and a few small pieces of wreckage spattered against his suit. He heard rather than felt them, but two larger chunks turned the situation into disaster.

The first hit with a dull clang that rang through his suit. Tom felt the impact on the right control arm of his jets. He knew that meant deep trouble. He'd lost his fine-tuning controls, the ones that kept him from pitching or rolling as he flew through space.

Tom fought for control with the less precise left-hand equipment. The right-hand controls were dead. What if the oxygen line had been clipped? Pushing that unpleasant thought away, he jiggled the jet controls. He was still spinning wildly.

As he tumbled, Tom saw the ship, then the blast site, then the huge blue-and-white globe of Earth, then the distant silver-sheening Moon. They all passed in a slow, stately rotation. By sheer bad luck, he was facing the blast zone when the second piece of debris hit.

Tom not only felt this impact, he saw it. A sharp-edged piece of metal flew straight at his left eye. It smashed into the helmet bubble, lodging there. Tom stared in horror as a spiderweb of cracks appeared in the acrylic plastic. *Explosive decompression*. The words crashed in his brain.

If the bubble blew out, all the air would leave Tom's suit—and his body. He remembered a lurid sci-fi thriller he had seen, with a guy trapped unprotected on an airless planet. His eyes had popped, literally bursting out of his skull. His mouth had been torn open, his tongue out like a swollen sausage. Even then, Tom knew, they hadn't shown the worst part—the blood boiling out of the body in a cloud of reddish vapor. All that would soon happen to him if he didn't get back inside the pressurized hull of the ship.

He raised a gloved hand to the cracked plastic and realized the horrible trap he was in. The crack was on the left side of the bubble. If he used his left hand to contain the damage, he couldn't operate the jet control he needed to get back to *Moonstalker*. He could stretch his right hand across to the crack, but that would block his view. How could he see where he was going?

To make things worse, he was still tumbling out of control. As the ship passed before him again, he realized it looked smaller. He was drifting away!

His only other option was to try stretching his right hand across to the jet controls on the left side. Fighting the clumsy, bulky spacesuit material wouldn't be easy, but it was his only chance.

"Tom!" Captain Nelson barked over the radio. "What's wrong?"

"Big problems," Tom explained. "I'm going to try jetting back in, but I may need help."

"The professors are already suited up, examining the cube. I'll have Sue prepare the MMU. Domovoy has trained on it. He can fly out and help you." Tom knew that the scientist wouldn't be much help against a blowout. He'd just be bringing back a dead body. Tom *had* to get to *Moonstalker* before he lost his air!

Straining, he reached his hand across his chest. He could just reach the jet controls. Tom forced his body to roll around, then fired a few short bursts. With agonizing slowness, he managed to stabilize himself.

In the distance floated the supershuttle. *Moonstalker* was more than two hundred feet long, but it looked very small and far away.

Tom triggered his jet in short, stuttering bursts, heading back toward the spaceship. His progress was painfully slow, but he feared that stronger blasts would send him out of control. As it was, he faced a complicated balancing act.

"Tom, Domovoy is on his way," Captain Nelson reported. Now Tom was close enough to see movement in the shuttle's cargo bay. There was a spacesuited figure, with the bulky MMU on its back. Moments later, Professor Domovoy was flying toward him.

"Do you hear me?" the professor's accented voice crackled in Tom's earphones.

"Loud and clear," Tom told him.

"I'll jet behind you. When I say so, you cut your thrust." The professor wasn't trying for fuel economy. He was moving at a fair clip as he passed Tom. "Okay! Cut it!" he yelled.

Tom released his controls. A moment later, he felt the impact as the jet-propelled Domovoy rammed into him, pushing him toward *Moonstalker*.

For a terrifying second, Tom feared that the shock had shattered his helmet. More cracks appeared. But Domovoy pushed Tom toward the supershuttle much faster than Tom's damaged jet could.

Stopping would be the real nightmare, Tom realized. Even the mildest additional strain could cause his cracked helmet to shatter. The only good part, he noticed, was that the airlock door was already open.

Domovoy cleverly swung around in front of Tom to cushion their deceleration. But even the gentle jarring of slowing down was too much for the weakened faceplate. As they put down in the cargo bay, Tom heard the hiss of escaping air.

"It's giving way!" he yelled into the radio, as he plunged for the airlock. He had time for one deep breath as he landed in the cylinder. Then his helmet burst outward in a thousand fragments. Tom didn't see it. He had his eyes shut tight, mouth clenched, a hand groping to cover his nose.

Terrible cold washed over his face, and his throat lurched as air tried to escape his lips and nose. Tom's temples pounded, and there was a roaring in his ears, which popped alarmingly. Blind, his eyes squeezed tight against a pressure that threatened to pop them from their sockets, he could only hope that the airlock door had closed behind him and that air was being pumped in.

How long would he have to wait? Could he count his heartbeats? No. His heart was thudding as if he were trying to run a one-minute mile. Stars of pain exploded behind his eyelids. Still he held on, trying to hold his breath against steadily increasing pressure.

Finally it burst free. Tom heard something like a strangled cough as his lungs emptied. Then it hit him. He'd *heard* it! There was enough atmosphere in the chamber to hear! His chest pumped, sucking in the thin air.

He opened his clenched eyes. For a second, a red haze obscured his vision, then his eyes cleared. A cloud of acrylic plastic shards floated around him. Scanning them carefully, he clumsily managed to scoop up the fragment of debris that had nearly killed him. It was a chunk of metal equipment casing with a piece of circuit board attached. In the corner of the board was a logo—a pair of stylized thunderbolts in the shape of a T.

The airlock hatch swung open to reveal Sue Chong's concerned face. "Tom! Are you—?"

Tom collapsed into her arms. That was the last he remembered for a while.

The next thing Tom knew, he woke to find himself zipped into one of the middeck bunk beds. He undid the covers and bumbled over to the personal hygiene station to look in the mirror. Bloodshot eyes, a face puffy and peeling and a little pale stared back at him. Returning to the common room, he bumped into Sue.

"So, you're alive." A relieved smile played over her face. "You didn't miss much. The professors are both out in the cargo bay, still fussing over the cube."

They climbed to the flight deck to listen to the scientists arguing on the radio. "This surface was made in vacuo," Packard said. "Obviously, this was created in space."

"They've been arguing in Latin since they went out there," Neal Tyrone told them.

Tom got on the mike. "Professor Packard, I suggest you drill a core sample, seal it, and examine it in here. I think you'll find traces of Earth gases trapped inside the rock."

There was a moment of offended silence from the usually jovial professor. "And how, may I ask, did you come to this theory?" Packard asked.

"Fact: whoever left that cube also left the

watchdog satellite that blew up," Tom said. "The piece that nearly killed me bears the logo of Takashima Electronics. So, Professor, unless the little green men are buying circuit boards on Earth, the satellite and the cube came from our planet and nowhere else."

The professor was silent for a while. When he spoke again, his voice was thoughtful. "How do we explain the vacuum vitrification?"

Tom shrugged. "Anyone with a vacuum chamber and a laser could have done the job on Earth," he said. "They'd just have to keep the cube stored in a vacuum until it was launched." He thought for a second. "Or if they had a space shuttle, they could do the job up here."

"But NASA has the only space shuttles!" Sue protested.

"The Soviets had shuttles under development," Tom pointed out. "We know they've run unmanned tests. But at present, with the way they've been selling off parts of their space program . . ."

"Anyone could have bought their shuttle." Chuck Nelson's strong-featured face grew grave.

Tom turned to the captain. "I think we should talk with the people on the ground—on the secure line."

Nelson nodded and began pushing controls. Other shuttles, flying secret defense missions, had used secure links to Ground Control—communications that were not open to the media. The secure line on *Moonstalker* was encoded by the best equipment Swift Enterprises could build. It led not to Mission Control, but to Frederick Napier's private office. Rick Cantwell, Mr. Swift, or Napier himself were to take turns monitoring the secure audio-video link.

All of them were in the office when Tom called down. After hearing the story, Mr. Swift stared grimly at the logo on the shard in Tom's hand. "Takashima, eh? We've had some run-ins with them. Yuri Takashima runs his company more like a pirate ship than a technology conglomerate."

"Harlan Ames has told me about some corporate espionage problems lately," Tom said.

"Takashima has a reputation for selling military high tech to anyone who meets his price," Frederick Napier put in. "That includes terrorist regimes and, at the height of the cold war, the Soviets. But then, Takashima *is* half Russian."

Aboard *Moonstalker*, Tom and Sue exchanged glances. Here was a link to the country with the only other operating space shuttle system.

"How does a Eurasian wind up running a big Japanese company?" Nelson asked. "I thought foreigners had a tough time doing business there."

"Arm twisting, leg breaking, head bashing—do I need to draw a picture?" Mr. Swift asked. "Takashima made alliances with yakuza gangster leaders to take over small electronics firms. When the Japanese government became interested, he went offshore, gobbling up companies all around the Pacific Rim. Even Swift Enterprises has fended off takeover feelers from Takashima."

"Nice guy," Rick Cantwell said.

"Oh, he's a charmer, all right," Mr. Swift agreed. "But why set up this orbiting puzzle box? What can he hope to gain from it?"

"The drawings on the cube direct us to the Moon," Tom reminded his father. "We've got the fuel and equipment to check out the Hertzsprung Crater."

Tom took a deep breath. "If the bad guys are really up to something out here, I think we should know."

9

GROUND CONTROL TO MAJOR TOM ..." THE old rock song echoed from the speakers of *Moonstalker*'s radio system. It was the morning of the second day since the supershuttle had left Earth orbit for its new destination—the Moon.

Tom Swift had drawn the upright sleeping bag set against the wall instead of a bunk. In microgravity, sleeping "standing up" was just as comfortable as sleeping "lying down." The blaring music brought him awake with a start.

"Hey, guys," a familiar voice came over the speakers. "It's your earthbound astronaut pal, Allie McVeigh, with your wake-up call. Is Tom Swift up and about?"

At that moment, Tom was wriggling into a set of blue coveralls. He unzipped the sleeping bag and slipped out, fully dressed. Floating up to the hatch to the flight deck, he quickly ran a hand through his rumpled blond hair. Let's hope I don't look *too* horrible if I have to go on TV, he told himself.

Upstairs, Neal Tyrone was sitting in the duty seat. "Here he is now," he said, grinning at Tom.

There was a short but noticeable delay before Allie said hello. Tom knew that although radio waves travel at the speed of light, the farther *Moonstalker* flew from Earth, the longer it took for messages to arrive. He grinned when he heard Allie's greeting. "So they've decided to pretty up the Mission Control desk this morning, eh?" he teased.

Allie laughed. "Right. The TV cameras will be in a little later, so we want you guys up and dressed." She stared at Tom. "What happened to your face?"

Although Tom had come through the effects of having his helmet faceplate blow out pretty well, he had one souvenir from facing the cold of space with his unprotected skin. Skin was peeling off his face as if he had a bad sunburn. He raised a hand, brushing at some of the loose skin. "Tension, I guess. Just don't put me in any close-ups. So what's our schedule for the day?"

"As if you didn't know, you're going into lunar orbit." Allie's voice became a bit wistful. "I wish I were along for that." Then her voice grew brisker, more businesslike. "We have some unofficial visitors this morning, too."

"Tom!" That was Mr. Swift's voice.

"Long time no hear." Rick Cantwell's voice came over loud and clear.

Tom grinned, sensing the fine hand of his father at work. They had talked only the day before, but on the secure communications link. No one knew about that, and this little acting scene had been set up for the benefit of the media—and whoever was behind the orbiting hoax they had picked up.

"We'll be observing you until you pass out of communication," Tom's father said.

Tom nodded. *Moonstalker* had been aimed at a point slightly ahead of the Moon on its orbit. Soon the spacecraft's rockets would be fired to swing around into lunar orbit. They would pass around the far side of the Moon, and *Moonstalker* would be out of contact with Mission Control and everyone else on planet Earth.

"Actually, I've been thinking about that," Tom said. "I suggest establishing some sort of link while we're investigating the Hertzsprung Crater, on the far side."

"If we'd known we were going, we could have launched a communications satellite,"

Sue Chong said, pulling herself through the hatch.

"We still could," Tom told her.

"But only if we had a spare satellite transponder aboard," Neal Tyrone said. "And according to the cargo manifest, we don't."

"We have a sort-of crew member who could do the job," Tom pointed out. "Does the name Orb ring a bell?"

The round robot had spent most of the voyage being carried by Rob or sharing data with the shipboard computers. Now Rob brought Orb up to the flight deck. "Two things, Orb." Tom said. "Before we lifted off, I had you made spaceworthy, so cold or vacuum wouldn't damage you, right?"

"Yes, Tom," Orb replied.

"Could you be left out in space—say in an orbit around the Moon—without ill effects?"

"Of course." Orb hesitated for a second. "But if you intend to use me as a communications satellite, you should leave me in a geosynchronous orbit—one that always keeps me over the same portion of the Moon's surface. You would also have to boost my power."

"I'll take care of the second problem," Tom said. "Why don't you compute the calculations for your orbit?"

Down in Houston, the business of Mission Control swirled around the special visitors.

Mr. Swift and Rick Cantwell stood beside Allie McVeigh, staring at the video feed from *Moonstalker*. The star of the show was actually Orb, as customized for satellite duty by Tom. A band of jets scavenged from Tom's MMU now surrounded Orb's "equator." Tom had also added a pair of solar panels to the top and bottom of the silvery globe.

Allie turned from the screen. "Mr. Swift, your son is just amazing. You must be very proud of him."

"I am," Tom's father said.

"Yeah, Tom's a great guy," Rick said, smiling at Allie. "But I guess you would know that, after going through astronaut school with him."

Allie turned back to the screen without a word.

Rick shrugged. He'd tried making conversation with the college student twice before, only to have her act as if he had infectious dandruff. Well, three strikes and she's out, he told himself.

Still, when Allie excused herself a little while later, Rick found himself following her. He turned away, though, when he saw her stop at a pay telephone. Probably calling her boyfriend, he decided.

After lunch in the VIP dining room, Allie, Mr. Swift, and Rick returned for more hours of radio messages and occasional video feeds.

They watched as *Moonstalker* approached its rendezvous with the Moon.

It was a ticklish business. Rob would have to be deployed in geosynchronous orbit, and then the supershuttle would have to insert itself into lunar orbit.

The craft's video cameras followed Rob as he floated out of the airlock into the cargo bay and attached a tether line from his waist to a metal loop on the floor of the bay. Everyone at Mission Control watched as Rob carefully attached Orb to the Remote Manipulator Arm.

Captain Nelson slowed the craft, and Sue Chong operated the arm. The job went without a hitch. Orb was officially in orbit.

"Mission Control, do you read me?" Orb's voice sounded much more metallic than usual. Rick couldn't decide if that was due to the radio transmission or Orb's power boost.

Allie McVeigh was back as Ground Liaison, so she replied. "You're coming in loud and clear, Orb."

Captain Nelson ignited the Orbital Maneuvering System engines, sweeping the supershuttle into orbit. For the first time in more than twenty years, humans were mere miles away from the lunar surface. Awed gasps came from the crew at their first closeup views. "Look at those mountains!" Professor Packard breathed.

"Unbelievable!" Neal Tyrone exclaimed.

Every eye at Mission Control stared at the large video monitor showing the craggy gray-and-black face of the far side relayed by Orb. The stark, airless view gave Rick the shivers. He had to glance away. In doing that, he happened to glance at Allie McVeigh.

Oddly enough, she wasn't looking at the screen, either. Her eyes were on a desk computer networked into the control systems. They moved from the machine's disk drive to its keyboard. Allie punched a couple of keys, then turned her eyes back to the screen.

Rick's eyes flicked from the screen to the computer. The Engaged light on the disk drive was on. On the screen, *Moonstalker* passed over a knife-edged set of mountains. "Outrageo—" Tom's broadcasted voice began.

Then the screen on the wall went black. Cries erupted from all around the room as the staff turned its attention to suddenly malfunctioning hardware.

"What's going on?" Mr. Swift shouted over the hubbub.

"I don't know!" an infuriated staffer exploded, frantically tapping at his keyboard. "It's like a virus got into the system—but I never saw a virus work this quickly."

Whole sections of computers went down as chaos spread through the network. It wasn't just desk terminals, either. The big mission control computers began flashing distress signals. Before Rick's eyes, an entire bank of electronic brains went dark.

Glancing back toward the computer where he'd seen Allie, Rick noticed she was no longer there. He scanned the whole room, searching for a glimpse of red curls amid the confusion. There she was—near the exit!

Rick darted through chaos, dodging technicians moving from computer to computer. He didn't bother asking questions when he caught up to Allie—he just tackled her.

Behind them, the computer she'd tampered with suddenly blew up.

"That must have been some disk you stuck in there," Rick gasped.

The blast cut off the human noise in the room like a flipped switch. Only one voice continued, from a man with earphones on. *"Moonstalker,* come in! This is Ground Control! *Moonstalker!"*

He looked up in despair. "They're off the air!"

At a secret command post, technicians stared up from their work stations at a large-screen TV. Moments before, it had shown the surface of the Moon. Now a stunned-looking news commentator tried to fill in the on-air time.

"We, ah, seem to have lost the transmission

from the supershuttle *Moonstalker*." The vast talking head glanced frantically off-camera. "Ah, at the moment, there's no announcement from NASA's Houston Mission Control. In fact, they're not even answering their telephones."

The announcer shook his head, baffled. "Ladies and gentlemen, we apologize. The *Moonstalker* live lunar transmission was to have continued for another half hour. But it has now cut off, mere moments after the supershuttle passed around to the dark side of the moon."

From a command console overlooking all the other work stations, a man threw his head back and laughed.

Aboard *Moonstalker*, the discovery of the break in communications came 2.6 seconds later—the amount of time it took for a radio call to reach Earth and go unanswered.

Captain Chuck Nelson stared at the control panel. "Ground Control, come in," he repeated into the mike. He glanced over at Tom. "Looks as if your pet robot blew a gasket or something."

Frowning, Tom took the mike. "Orb, come in. Is there some sort of problem?"

A moment later, Orb's voice came over the speakers. "I read you loud and clear, Tom. But there are no transmissions coming from

Ground Control. I'm detecting bits of radio transmissions from all over Earth but not from Houston."

Sue Chong gasped. "You don't think it's an earthquake or something?"

"Oh, it's something, all right," Tom replied. "Something arranged by the people who put that cube in the sky." His frown grew deeper. "They have a longer reach than I imagined."

Nelson and Tyrone were frowning just as deeply. "Shouldn't we consider scrubbing the mission?" the captain said.

"We're already moving across the far side of the Moon," Tom pointed out. "Soon we'll be over the Hertzsprung Crater. At a hundred miles up, we should at least be able to get some fresh photos of the area—see if anything's there."

"We can do more than that," Packard promised. "Domovoy and I plan to run a full scan of the crater floor."

"You'd better get busy, then," Nelson said. "We'll be coming up on the crater pretty soon. And you're getting just one shot at it, because as soon as we get back to the other side, we're heading home."

The nose of the spacecraft pointed down, facing the pitted lunar surface. Staring out the flight deck windows, Tom saw the jagged wall of a crater pass directly below. Wind and water had never worn away the raw rock. And without the blurring effects of an atmosphere, the view of the crater rim was incredibly sharp. To Tom, the peak seemed right outside the window. Perhaps because of the Moon's smaller size, its whole surface seemed to curve outward at an exaggerated angle. It was like looking through a trick camera lens. Tom glanced away to where the professors stood at the imaging controls, swinging long-range cameras toward Hertzsprung.

Tom caught the image on a video screen. The crater was enormous, a monument to a catastrophic meteor impact. It was pockmarked with smaller craters, the results of later crashes, Tom knew. "Remember the map on the cube?" he asked the professors. "Why not try aiming for the spot indicated by that spider carving?"

Packard consulted for a moment with Domovoy, who suggested the coordinates. The image on the screens blurred, then steadied again.

"We're zeroing in," Packard reported.

Now the field of view shrank dramatically to a small section of the crater floor. Most of it was the already familiar grayish rock that seemed to form the Moon's surface. But in the middle of the picture was something that couldn't—*shouldn't*—have been there.

"Going for maximum enlargement," Packard said. The impossible object grew larger, springing into sharper focus.

"Somebody sure went to a lot of trouble," Tom muttered.

The object on the crater floor looked familiar to Tom. It reminded him of a bad special effect from a Japanese science fiction movie. Its overall appearance was spiderlike. Eight spindly "legs" stuck out at odd angles from a swollen "body" that rose about ten feet off the floor of the Hertzprung Crater. Each leg was about fifteen feet long, and Tom could see that the central portion had a strange hump on its top. From this angle, though, it was hard to identify what that might be.

Moments later, Moonstalker was directly over the crater. Tom glanced from the video screen to the windows but could see nothing on the gray surface below. On the screen, though, he saw that the object on top of the body was shaped like a sensor dish, and it was beginning to move.

"Captain!" Neal Tyrone suddenly spoke up. "We're getting some sort of transmission. No! It's a burst of static!"

Alarms began shrieking as the control board went wild.

"Not a burst of static," Tom corrected him, hurtling to one of the control computers. "It's an EMP—electromagnetic pulse—and it's on the exact wavelength of our computers."

The gauges on an entire flight console abruptly went dead.

"What—?" Sue Chong began.

"The military originally discovered the EMP problem," Tom explained. "Nuclear weapons sent off huge bursts of electromagnetic radiation, which destroyed sensitive electronic equipment. This pulse was smaller and more carefully aimed—just enough to destroy our computer controls."

As he spoke, more control gauges disappeared on the command console. Tom managed to slap one computer off before it blew. The others died in a crescendo of beeps and alarms as system failures cascaded.

When the din subsided, the crew was frozen in a moment of silence.

"It's over," Sue Chong finally said.

"Over for all of us." Captain Nelson's voice was hoarse. "That pulse did in four of our computers. Four out of five. We thought we had a safe redundancy with that many, but the problem is that we need *two* computers to fly this bird."

He pointed to the joystick on the dead command console. "Pulling that doesn't directly turn the ship. It just initiates a whole chain of computer-driven commands to the propulsion systems."

"But now we don't have the computers to control the rockets," Tom said heavily. "The machine we have left will maintain the environmental equipment and keep us alive."

Neal Tyrone's voice was as cold as space itself. "But it won't keep us flying. Our orbit is degrading—we're going to crash into the Moon!"

10

BACK IN HOUSTON, THE EMERGENCY LIGHTS flickered on at the entrance to the underground Mission Control room. A young guard gawked as the dim lighting revealed Allie McVeigh trying to escape Rick Cantwell's grasp. "Let go of me!" she yelled.

"What's going on here?" The young guard went for the pistol at his hip.

"If you want to find out, help me hold onto her. She was fooling around with the computer that suddenly made like the Fourth of July."

The confused guard helped Allie up but didn't let go of her arm. "Where should we take her?" he asked.

"How about Mr. Napier's office?" Rick suggested, starting down the hall. "I'm sure he'd like to hear what we have to say."

When Rick, Allie, and the guard stepped into the NASA administrator's office, they found Mr. Swift already there. Frederick Napier stood by the secure communications link, looking ready to explode. "The unscrambling equipment here is undamaged," he told Mr. Swift. "The problem is, transmissions come in through the Mission Control computers. The telephone may be fine, but it won't work if the switchboard has broken down."

He glared at the sudden interruption. "What's this? And what's *she* doing here?"

"I think you've got her to thank for the mess outside," Rick told him.

"That's not true!" Allie cried.

"I saw you at the pay phone after you learned that Tom was leaving Orb behind as a communications link," Rick said. "At the time, I thought you were just making an ordinary call. Now I think you were calling for instructions."

In spite of Allie's loud protests, Rick went on, telling what he'd seen during the last seconds of the supershuttle's passage to the far side of the Moon.

"You didn't actually see her put a disk in the machine?" Mr. Swift asked.

"No. Her hand was moving away from the disk drive when I first glanced over," Rick admitted. "But I definitely saw her input something on the keyboard."

"I just rested my hand there for a moment," Allie said desperately.

Mr. Swift turned to Napier. "I think you should have some specialists take a look at what's left of the computer."

"I agree." Napier picked up his phone, directing a ferocious glare at Allie even as he made the arrangements. "I'd just like to point out something you may not have thought of," he told her after he'd hung up. "This little stunt counts as destruction of federal property. That means the FBI will be in on this investigation."

Allie plunked wordlessly down on one of the office chairs. To Rick, she looked scared stiff, but he still saw a defiant gleam in her eye. The hostile silence continued for long minutes, until it was finally interrupted by the bleat of the telephone. Allie nearly jumped out of her skin.

"Napier," the NASA man said, picking up the phone. He listened for a moment, cocking an eyebrow. "I see. And you'll stand by those findings? Good."

He hung up the phone and swung on Allie. "My technical staff has discovered traces of an extremely sophisticated plastic explosive in the debris of the computer. Judging from the shape of the remaining fragments, they think it was inserted in the form of a three-and-a-half-inch floppy disk."

"A next-generation sabotage weapon," Mr. Swift said. "It's a bomb that actually accepts programming. Terrorists can poison a computer system and destroy all traces of how they did it. Not even fingerprints remain."

"If she hadn't moved away, not much of Allie would have remained, either," Rick added. "She would have been nearest to the blast."

Allie McVeigh's shoulders sagged, and her face went pale. "It has to be some kind of mistake," she said in a hollow voice. "This wasn't supposed to happen at all."

"Then what *was* supposed to happen?" Napier snapped. "Look, kid," he said when Allie didn't answer, "when the FBI gets on a case, they investigate in depth. Your teachers will get visits from Feds. So will your friends, your family . . ."

Tears spilled from Allie's eyes. "This was supposed to be the end of the—the—" she fumbled for a word. "Well, Mr. Ulrich called it 'the operation.'"

"And just who is this Mr. Ulrich?" Napier wanted to know.

Tom Swift, Sr., leaned close to Allie. "Describe Ulrich," he demanded.

"He—he's short, just a little taller than I am. Skinny, with an accent and blond hair—"

"Leon Ulrich, ex-head of technical services for GSG-Nine, the German antiterrorism agency. Fired when he was discovered moonlighting for German corporations. Now he free-lances in corporate espionage—and sabotage." Mr. Swift looked as if he'd just encountered a worm in his apple. "My chief of security, Harlan Ames, has tangled with him once or twice. Ulrich works for every dirty company, including, oddly enough, Takashima Electronics." He turned to Allie. "This time, though, he wasn't trying to get information out. He was trying to get someone *in*. I expect he first used you only to feed us a line."

Allie nodded. "He said it was a way to penetrate your security," she admitted. "Mr. Ulrich turned up after the Swift technicians came to the San Damian observatory and installed the extra power equipment for Tom's experiments. He knew he'd have no luck getting at the Swift people. So he went after the university people instead and got me. Ulrich knew all about what Tom was going to do and told me to volunteer as the research assistant. I was going to be a 'conduit,' he said."

She took a deep breath. "All I had to do was aim the telescope at certain coordinates he gave me. The rest, he said, would be done by Tom, Swift Enterprises, and NASA. They'd all go off looking to meet E.T.—and when the hunt was exposed as a hoax, they'd look pretty silly."

"If that's all you had to do, why are you here now?" Rick asked.

"Ulrich told me to go to the Swifts. At first I thought it was just a way to escape the media craziness. Then NASA picked Tom and me for training. For a little while, I even hoped to make the shuttle. But I wasn't smart enough. Still, I helped Tom." Allie hung her head. "I felt like a louse, setting him up to be embarrassed. I like him."

"Sure, that's why you sabotaged his mission," Rick said sarcastically.

"This is about much more than embarrassment." Frederick Napier's voice was solemn. "I've heard rumbles in the government—especially the White House staff—about privatizing space. The idea is to take the burden off NASA's shoulders by letting private businesses take over rocket launches and satellite deployments."

His face grew even redder. "But there's a clear danger. A gutted space program would leave the field open for a few ruthless types to take over the High Frontier. With a monopoly over space travel, they'd have a stranglehold on humanity's future."

Napier shrugged. "Hey, I don't say we're angels, but NASA's goals don't include making a profit off the back of everyone on

Earth." He sighed. "Lately, though, we've found ourselves fighting for our lives against polls, national media attacks, and political pressure—a carefully orchestrated campaign."

"The only problem is, we don't know who's waving the baton," Mr. Swift said. He turned to Allie. "Unless *you* can tell us."

She raised a tear-stained face. "I—I don't know. The disk was only a kind of joke, not a—a bomb." She shook her head, still recovering from her near brush with death. "My only contact with any of this was Mr. Ulrich, and he didn't say much." She frowned, thinking. "He once mentioned that he represented a consortium of companies. That was how he got me into the whole deal. One was this big Far Eastern electronics company. Their Silicon Valley subsidiary pays for my research fellowship. If I didn't go along, they'd cut me off."

"Was that all?" Mr. Swift asked.

"That was the stick. They also offered me a carrot. If I did well, there was another company building a huge observatory on a Pacific Island. They could offer me a position after I finished school. And what I had to do seemed so small, so unimportant—"

"How does blowing out NASA's computer system seem so innocent?" Rick wanted to know.

Allie finally cracked wide open, tears

streaming down her face. "I told you, that wasn't supposed to happen. I'd been given a computer disk to slip into the system when *Moonstalker* went behind the Moon. When I typed in the command, a program would fill every screen with full details about the hoax."

She looked desperately at the other people in the room. "That's all that was supposed to happen. When I heard that Tom would still have a radio link, I called Ulrich, and he said go ahead."

Allie McVeigh's voice rose. "What would *you* have done? I'd lose my scholarship. I tried to get out before this, but Ulrich told me I was in too deep. And I swear to you, *I didn't think I was doing anything so bad!* Something must have gone disastrously wrong!"

"What went wrong was that you trusted scum," Mr. Swift said. "This is what Ulrich and whoever is behind him intended all along. Announcing a hoax would have made us look silly, or maybe incompetent. But chasing a hoax—and then losing a shuttle and crew— that would mean the end of any government space program and the end of Swift Enterprises in space, as well. Perhaps you didn't know that before, Ms. McVeigh. I hope you understand now."

Napier called in the young guard, who had

remained outside the office. "Take her away. This girl is going to jail."

Silently, tears still running down her face, Allie let herself be led off.

Napier rubbed his face, which now looked haggard from strain. "Well, I have a space mission to manage," he finally said, rising from his desk. "Let's get back out on the floor and see what's going on."

The regular lights were back on in Mission Control as they stepped into the cavernous room. Rick saw that the screens on the massed data terminals were also flickering with light. In fact, the whole place looked normal—except for the worried looks on all the controllers' faces.

"Still no luck, sir," the control director reported when he saw Napier. "The hardware is mostly up and running, but we haven't heard a word from *Moonstalker* since everything blew up."

"Okay. The other side has been ahead of us all the way. And as far as we know, all their plans have worked out perfectly." Tom Swift, Sr.'s, face set in hard lines. Part of the enemy's plans included the death of his son.

"I only wish we knew what was happening on the far side of the Moon!"

11

THREE HOURS LEFT, TOPS," TOM SWIFT MUT-
tered. He was a quarter of a million miles
away from Earth, aboard the doomed *Moonstalker*, resting cross-legged on the flight deck.
Beside him hunkered Rob, who still func-
tioned. The electromagnetic pulse that had
knocked out the computers had been set to a
specific frequency—one that didn't affect him.
Rob's mechanical help was invaluable as the
crew picked through the mass of electrical
components they'd assembled in plastic bags.

No one looked out the forward windows at
the passing landscape of the Moon. The peaks
that had fascinated them earlier seemed too
close for comfort now.

"System Three CPU," Rob said, running a

trickle current through the circuit board of a crashed computer. "Some memory chips are okay, but the microprocessors are all burned out."

"Great," Tom said bitterly. "We've got memory to burn, but the guts of the system, the chips we really need, have all been fried."

"Tom," Rob said, "I think that was the idea. That EMP was on a specific frequency. It blew a lot of stuff, but it was really aimed at the processors."

"In that case, whoever set up the phony alien spaceship down there did a perfect job." Tom moodily picked out another circuit board, checked it, and tossed it into a plastic bag filled with similar debris. "Let's face it, the bad guys did a real job on us. First they suckered us behind the Moon, then they cut us off from Earth, and finally blew out most of our controls. Unless we can restore one computer with parts from the four that crashed . . ."

"I know—we'll crash, too." Rob's photocell eyes glowed for a second.

"By then, we'll be back on the visible side of the Moon. Anybody with a halfway decent telescope should be able to pick out where we go down."

"Shut up!" Professor Packard exploded. His cheerful self had disappeared with the announcement of their doom. "We're going to die! We may as well give up!"

"*You* shut up, Alvin." Instead of gloom, concentrated purpose gleamed in Professor Domovoy's face. "Help me sort these circuits. We can beat this situation—if we *work*." He handed another relatively undamaged board to Rob.

Sue Chong and Neal Tyrone glared at Packard until he rejoined them at work. They had a tough job, hunting through the dead computers for usable circuitry and chips. They all faced an inflexible deadline. Only if the whole crew worked together did they have any chance of survival.

Tom tossed another useless circuit board into a plastic bag. "We have to come up with another computer, Rob. Without a pair of controlling systems, *Moonstalker* is even less flyable than the first generation of shuttles."

"The ones they called 'falling refrigerators' because of the rough way they landed?" Rob asked.

"Hey, they came down really steep, but at least they had an atmosphere to land in," Tom pointed out. "There's no air on the Moon to break our fall—just rock to get smashed on." He shook his head. "We've *got* to come up with something."

Rob stowed yet another useless board. "I

know, boss. Where's a Cheapo Chips and Circuit Shop when you need it?"

"About two hundred fifty thousand miles away," Tom said in disgust. "A little too far to walk."

"I'd give up my own CPU chips, but you said they didn't have the juice," Rob said.

Tom sighed, discarding yet another burnt-out set of circuits. "If we're going to wish ourselves out of this squeeze, why piddle around with a few chips? Why not wish for a replacement computer system? It's just as far away as . . ."

His voice trailed off. Then he hit himself in the forehead with the palm of his hand. "Rob, I think getting stuck without air in that spacesuit must have killed a few brain cells. We *do* have a replacement computer system, fairly nearby."

"We do?" Captain Nelson whirled around, nearly smacking his head on the case of the computer he was disassembling.

"Sure we do!" Tom sprang to his feet so fast, he forgot about the microgravity on board the shuttle. He bounced off the ceiling before he could stop himself, but he was grinning as he floated back down. "It's in geosynchronous orbit, dropped off by our remote manipulator arm."

"Orb?" Sue's voice was questioning.

"Orb! The brains to my brawn!" Rob burst

out. "That's right! That's no brainless communications satellite. Orb is chock-full of microprocessors."

Tom frowned in thought. "The only problem is, how do we get back together with Orb again? We'll crash before we make it back to his position." He began sorting through the discarded wiring. "We've got to do this as quickly as possible. Sue, find me a power line. Professors, can you find me a working circuit that leads to a transmitter array?"

Even as he spoke, Tom was already laboring, cobbling together a safe coupling that would boost Rob's power without burning any more precious chips. Rob and Orb were built to be always in communication. Therefore, if Tom could boost Rob's transmission, they could talk to Orb!

Rob wound up resting on the floor beside Neal Tyrone's seat, his chest panel opened up and a mass of lead wires stretching into the opened console. The whole crew stared intently at the console speaker.

"Rob . . . *Moonstalker!*" Orb's metallic voice seemed a little rougher than usual. "I am glad to discover that the sudden break in our communication was not fatal to you all." The orbiting computer paused as Rob quickly ran a concentrated message on their situation.

"If you are to survive this computer breakdown, you must have me aboard before you collide with the lunar surface." Orb went off the line for agonizing seconds. "I calculate that by using all my reaction mass, I should be able to rendezvous with *Moonstalker* before you fall low enough to impact the higher lunar peaks."

"Then do it!" Captain Chuck Nelson burst out.

"I have initiated the sequence," Orb responded. "However, there is one concern. To reach you in time, I will have no fuel available for course corrections on arrival. I cannot land in *Moonstalker*'s cargo bay."

"You mean—?" Sue Chong's voice wobbled as she spoke.

"I shall have to be caught—by the remote manipulator system."

Moonstalker fell silently through the airless space surrounding the Moon. No one on board could even tell they were moving, much less dropping steadily closer to the Moon's surface. The only hint of motion was the shifting lunar panorama as seen through the flight deck windows. Tom Swift looked up and recognized Mare Tranquilitas—the Sea of Tranquility, where the first Apollo astronauts had landed.

I could use a little tranquility right now, he thought, wiping sweat out of his burning eyes. Did the bulging gray belly of the Moon seem closer?

He pushed the question away, turning his attention back to the interface circuits he was building. All the working memory circuits had been wired in, and the whole jury-rigged assembly had been patched to the control circuits. Tom had tested out some programming on the remaining computer. The linkage algorithms were virtually identical to Orb's programming. His suggestion to Dr. de Spain might just save their lives.

Tom could wire Orb into this electronic nightmare through the modifications he'd made to turn the silvery computer into a communications satellite. That left only one problem.

Before they could do anything with Orb, they had to catch him.

Tom looked over toward the aft control station, where Sue Chong and Rob were checking the remote manipulator controls, circuit by circuit. Professors Packard and Domovoy stood by with the sacks of scavenged electronics. Whenever Sue or Rob found damaged printed circuits or burnt-out wires, the scientists dug in to produce replacements.

Taking a deep breath, Tom glanced at his chronometer. Sue would even have a little time to test the arm before the moment of rendezvous. Then it would be down to plain luck.

"The arm is moving fine," Sue reported,

working with the joystick. "The camera at the end of the arm is transmitting perfectly." She put the robot arm through its paces with growing confidence.

Rob had already gone through the airlock and into the cargo bay, tethered himself, and installed the net they had used to snag the orbiting rock cube. The hoax cube was now tied down in a corner of the payload area, forgotten.

Chuck Nelson and Neal Tyrone were also at the aft station, shaking their heads and running programs on the computer. "Sorry, Sue," Tyrone finally said. "We don't dare try to use any of the reaction control systems to maneuver the ship to help you. They might fling us too far away or worse, steer us even faster toward the surface."

Nelson nodded. "Until we have two computers working, we just don't have control of this bird."

Sue Chong nodded, trying not to show the pressure Tom knew she must be feeling.

"I am now decelerating." Orb's voice came louder over the speaker. The robotic brain was very close to them now. The Moon's surface was very close, too. Jagged mountain peaks seemed to pass just below *Moonstalker*'s nose.

None of the crew members looked out the

shuttlecraft windows. All attention was on Sue Chong. The young astronaut had her feet firmly planted in microgravity shoe attachments. Dark sweat patches marked her blue coverall. Her tight, finely carved face gleamed with sweat as well. But her hand was steady as she gripped the joystick control.

"Fuel exhausted," Orb reported. "I have slowed enough, however, to give you an extra twenty seconds, Sue."

Great, Tom thought. She's got another twenty seconds to swing that arm around and catch Orb. If she misses, we're all dead.

He bit the inside of his lip. Of course, he told himself, if she grabs too hard, she may damage Orb. We'll have him, but we'll still be dead.

Finally, Tom stared only at Sue's hand on the joystick, not at the video screen showing the view from space. Sue shifted, sped the arm up, turned, made a tiny adjustment—and pulled the grapple trigger.

"Got it!" she cried.

The five other people aboard the shuttle released the breath they'd been holding.

Rob was already outside in the cargo bay, waiting to bring Orb in. The crew moved to its maneuvering stations. Tom made a last-minute check on the harness he'd set up to hold Orb securely inside one of the gutted computer cabinets.

They'd know soon enough if this would work.

Rob climbed into the flight deck, the chill of space still radiating off him. Orb was even colder, frost coating its silver metal skin.

"Don't touch yet, Tom," Rob warned. "Your fingers would stick."

Tom let Rob's metal hands remove the exterior additions he had attached to Orb. He busied himself with preparations, trying not to look at the watch on his wrist or the view out the windows.

"My surface temperature should be acceptable now," Orb said.

While Rob strapped Orb in place, Tom made the necessary circuit connections. Were his fingers shaking from the cold still radiating off Orb?

He fumbled for a second, making the last linkage. Then it was done. Had it worked?

For a second, nothing happened. Then lights returned to the command consoles.

"All right, people," Captain Nelson said. "Strap in!"

Tom took his place, and Rob scrambled downstairs.

The straps seemed very heavy on Tom's tight shoulders. We'll know in a second, he told himself. Either we're a spaceship again— or we're dead meat!

CAPTAIN CHUCK NELSON TAPPED THE AUTOPI-
lot panel for a roll maneuver using the RCS—
reaction control system—and grasped the
joystick.

Now we'll know if we have our controls
back, Tom thought. If Orb and the other
computer can't work together, we'll start
tumbling.

The course correction rockets fired, and the
Moon disappeared from view. Tom breathed
a sigh of relief to see stars through the windows. Nelson triggered the heavier Orbital
Maneuvering System. Rocket thrust pushed
Tom into his seat. The captain sat back, scanning the instruments. "We're two hundred
miles out, in a stable orbit."

"Way to go, Cap," Sue Chong cheered.

"Oh, it's not all wonderful," Nelson said. "That little rolling operation sent us in the opposite direction from the one we'd been traveling. We're going back behind the Moon. And without Orb out there as a communications link, we'll be in radio silence, whether our jury-rigged system works or not."

Tom was up, heading for the computer consoles. "But at least we're out of immediate danger. I'd like to run some diagnostic tests to make sure our computers are working together a hundred percent."

Nelson nodded. "Being only three percent off on a two-hundred-fifty-thousand-mile journey would still leave us seventy-five hundred miles away from home."

The tests, however, showed no problems. "All systems are now optimal," Orb reported. "Including communications."

From the console speaker, they heard a man with a twangy voice calling, "*Moonstalker*, this is Mission Control. *Please* come in."

"That's Everett Reese," Nelson told the crew. "We went through astronaut training together."

"I wonder what happened to Allie McVeigh," Tom said. He intercepted Nelson's hand at the transmit button. "Are you sure we should do that?"

The captain looked at him. "I think we should send out a broad-band announcement to tell the world that we're alive and heading home."

"The world includes the people who nearly killed us with that booby trap on the far side of the Moon," Tom pointed out. "I don't know if we should be telling them to try again."

"So what do you want to do?" Nelson asked.

"Why don't we use the secure link to Mr. Napier's office?" Tom suggested. "We could bounce our transmission off a communications satellite so nobody knows where it came from. The bad guys are obviously dangerous and clever. If they think we're dead, we may be able to smoke them out, with the help of NASA and my father."

He looked around at his fellow crew members. "Lastly, I think we should make one more orbit around the Moon, so we can visit the Hertzsprung Crater."

"What for?" Sue Chong wanted to know. "Why can't we just go home?"

"To salvage whatever we can from the phony alien object. We need to collect evidence," Tom said. "Whoever left that glorified bug zapper down there didn't expect us to survive. That means we may find clues as to who manufactured it."

Sue stubbornly shook her head. "That will

keep until NASA arranges another expedition. After all, we've got the only shut— Oh, no.''

"The only working space shuttles?" Tom gave her a smile without any humor. "We don't know that for sure anymore. What I think, though, is that somebody wants to drive NASA out of the shuttle business. What better way than to arrange a splashy mission where no one comes back?"

He shook his head. "I can just see the supermarket tabloid headlines: 'Crew Abducted by UFO Aliens!' But that would be the least of it. Think of how people debated continuing the shuttle program after *Challenger* blew up. And that was when NASA still had three other shuttles. There's only one *Moonstalker*. What do you think the public—and Congress—will do if we never show up again?"

"The program would be dead," Nelson said. He began working on the computers. "Problem is, there's no communications satellite available to bounce our signal off. The last of the old Syncom series finally broke down, and we haven't been able to launch a replacement." He glanced helplessly at Tom. "That was supposed to be one of our initial missions."

"So we have three hours before we can tell anyone we're all right," Tom said, quickly calculating how long it would take them to come out from behind the Moon. "Well, that gives me lots of time to check out Hertz-sprung—if I can get the Swift auxiliary lander ready."

"You're going down there?" Sue broke in.

"The lander is a two-person craft. One of those passengers has to be Rob, since he's programmed to pilot it." Tom shrugged. "And again, I'm the expendable member of the crew."

"Right," Sue agreed, deadpan. "Real expendable. We'd have been smeared halfway across the Moon without you."

"But you don't need me to operate the shuttle or to get back."

"He has a point," Nelson said. "Do it."

"Right." Sue went to get Tom's spacesuit, muttering, "Some people have all the luck."

She stopped in the hatchway to the mid-deck. "Hey! What are you going to use for a helmet?"

"Use the helmet from my suit," Professor Domovoy offered. "I'm not going anywhere."

Soon Tom and Rob were out in the vacuum of space, checking out the Swift auxiliary lander. It had been included as an after-thought, on the vague chance they might have to visit the Moon. Despite its name, *Moonstalker* was not designed to land and lift off from the airless satellite. That was the auxiliary lander's job.

Tom hid a smile as he looked at the craft.

The lander was almost the complete opposite of *Moonstalker*. Where the shuttlecraft was big and sleek, the lander was—well, klutzy-looking. Tall and gangly, it looked like something a kid had built using an Erector Set— an Erector Set with thin metal struts.

The lander's design called for no streamlining, because it was built to operate in airless conditions. The lander was just a rocket engine bolted to a metal framework. There were open positions where the pilot and a passenger could strap in, and storage modules—big boxes—that could be used to transport things down or bring them up.

In this case, the lander would go down empty and, Tom hoped, return with some backup computer components—and maybe some clues as to who had set up the lunar trap.

"Strapped in, boss?" Rob asked from the pilot's position.

"Ready," Tom replied.

"We read you," Nelson's voice crackled over Tom's earphones. "Preparing to release Lunar Lander *Nestor*."

Tom grinned. Trust Nelson to be so formal and use the name Tom Swift, Sr., had picked for the lander—Tom's mother's maiden name.

"RCS ignition," Nelson warned. The attitude control rockets fired, tilting *Moonstalker*'s nose downward. The cradle holding

Nestor in place rose up, and then the lander was floating free of its mother ship.

When they were well free of the spacecraft, Rob triggered the decelerators, allowing them to sink below *Moonstalker*'s orbit.

"We expect you to lift off within two hours and rejoin us before we come out of the Moon's radio shadow." Nelson repeated the time limit they'd agreed upon. Although Tom had enough air to allow *Moonstalker* to make a complete lunar orbit, they'd agreed to keep the landing expedition brief.

Rob used the steering jets, swinging them just to the east of center at the Hertzsprung Crater, near the fake artifact. The pock-marked ground seemed to rush up at them. For a second, Tom remembered the lunar lander computer game he'd played as a kid. Now he was doing it for real, twenty years after the last human visitors had left the Moon.

The lander's legs were now aimed at the ground. Rob triggered the decelerating jets, aiming for a clear stretch of long-frozen lava.

They touched down with a noticeable jolt, flexing the shock absorbers in the lander's legs. Quickly Tom unstrapped himself, but Rob was down ahead of him. "A large step for robotkind," Rob's voice rang in Tom's earphones.

"Quit clowning and let's take a look at that machinery," Tom said.

Seen up close, Tom felt the impressive "alien probe" looked downright phony. The bizarre design elements had been quickly welded onto the necessary power and transmitting equipment for the electromagnetic burst.

Tom laughed. The base of the construction was quite recognizable under the tacked-on chrome. It was from an old NASA lunar lander! "I remember seeing pictures of some of the landers in junkyards," he said. "Sort of like stealing NASA's old cheese to bait a trap for *Moonstalker*."

"How did they get it here?" Rob wondered.

"People have been soft-landing robots on the Moon since the Russians did it in 1966," Tom said. "This thing could have gone up disguised as a weather satellite or something. It probably disconnected from its final fuel stage and dropped here as programmed, waiting to zap us."

He examined the machinery on the phony probe. "Just as I thought. Generating that pulse drained its batteries. Let's see what circuitry we can scavenge—aha!"

"What is it?" Rob asked.

Tom held up the circuit board he'd removed from the now-dead booby trap, pointing at the crossed lighting bolts. "Takashima

Electronics strikes again. I'm beginning to suspect that they researched and developed this whole trap."

He and Rob walked back and forth from the derelict craft to their lander, carrying armloads of scavenged electronic gear. "We'll be able to rig a few more backup circuits now," Tom said.

The path to and from their vehicle passed over solid rock. Tom noticed that the surface dust had been swept away by the lander's rocket exhaust.

"We're finished way early," Rob said as he carried the last load. "Anything else we want to do while we're down here?"

Tom grinned. "Bring over the video camera."

He headed off the blasted rock for the huge expanse of Moondust that stretched all around them. "Start filming, Rob," Tom said. "I want a record of me leaving footprints on the Moon."

The dust was deeper than he expected. His foot sank down several inches, in a spray of flying particles.

"Careful, Tom," Rob called. "I don't want you sinking out of sight."

Walking carefully, Tom left several sets of widely spaced tracks. Rob followed him into the dust, then suddenly froze.

"What's the matter, Rob?" Tom asked, noticing his robot's strange pose.

"I'm feeling a tingle in my skin." Tom had installed sensors in Rob's outer metal covering to detect electrical charges.

"You mean, you're feeling an electrical trickle?" Tom asked.

"More like a resonating field." Rob bent over, his photocell eyes carefully observing his feet buried in the dust. "Look at your footprints, Tom."

Immediately Tom saw what the robot meant. The top layer of lunar dust was a dirty gray. But his footprints were a brilliant, almost glowing white!

Tom scooped up a handful of the mysterious dust. Looking closer, he saw it wasn't like sand. Each grain was a separate, glowing, perfect little crystal. "What *is* this stuff?"

"I don't know," Rob admitted. "But it's spread in a miles-wide circle. And whatever is generating the field I'm detecting lies smack in the middle of the circle of crystals— at the exact center of the crater."

"Do we have time to walk there?" Tom asked.

"I don't know about you," the robot answered, "but *I* could make it."

"Suppose you carried a passenger piggy-back," Tom said.

Before setting off, Tom relayed the situation to Captain Nelson and the *Moonstalker* crew. He and Rob also filled the lander's remaining cargo modules with the shining crystal dust.

Tom wished he could have gotten a shot of himself flying along the lunar landscape on Rob's shoulders. The robot ran in great bounding leaps, sailing tirelessly through a gravity one-sixth of Earth's. Thanks to the charge in the mysterious particles underfoot, he knew exactly how deep the dust layer was, even the contours of the surface beneath.

Following the resonating field, Rob easily homed in on its center. It was just a higher lump in the dust field. But as Tom brushed away the accumulation, that lump was revealed as a much larger version of the white crystals they'd found. Where the small ones were the size of grains of sand, this crystal was as big as Tom's head.

He picked the crystal up. It seemed to glow with a pulsing inner light, but it wasn't transparent. Tom dimly made out the outlines of different structures inside, structures almost too regular to be natural. He stared, entranced by the gleaming stone.

"Whoever set up that alien hoax chose better than they knew," Tom said in a hoarse voice. "They picked Hertzsprung Crater for their little game because it was on the lunar equator, and on the far side of the Moon. Funny. If they'd come down in person instead of sending an automated craft, they'd have discovered the real thing."

He held out the crystal to Rob. "This is no Hollywood imitation. It's the product of a high technology I know nothing about. Somebody—or some*thing*—left it here a long, long time ago."

"Some*thing*?" Rob repeated.

"It didn't have to be little green men. A robot probe could have spread the little crystals and deposited this. On the gray rock, the circle would have been a shining beacon. At least, it would have been before later impacts covered it with gray dust and debris." Inside his helmet, Tom shook his head. "But it happened way before that booby trap landed."

"How can you be sure, Tom?" Rob asked.

"There's no wind or air on the Moon," Tom said. "The gray dust has lain here since it settled from meteor impacts millions of years ago."

He stared almost reverently at the crystal in his hands. "When this was laid down, the highest life-forms on Earth were dinosaurs!"

13

THE TRIP BACK TO THE *NESTOR* WAS SLOWER than the journey out.

Again Tom rode astride Rob's polished metal shoulders. Rob held the crystal they'd discovered in both hands, as if he were carrying a giant eggshell.

"Wait till Professor Packard sees *this* Moon rock," Tom said. "He'll probably toss that phony-baloney carved cube over the side of the cargo bay." He thought for a second. "You know, this thing has been in vacuum for millions of years. Who knows what will happen if we expose it to air. We should probably keep it in the cargo bay, then seal it in a vacuum box before we land."

The *Nestor*'s flight back up to orbit was

quick and uneventful. Packed in glowing dust, the crystal rode in the lander's safest cargo module.

"This is going to be tricky," Rob said over the radio. "Nobody has ever gotten back *into* that cradle."

Captain Chuck Nelson's voice cut in. "Bring the *Nestor* in above the cargo bay, Rob, then cut thrust. We'll transfer everything with the remote arm."

Tom was the first to ride down on the cherry picker, the big crystal cradled in his arms. Then Rob rode several times, to deposit the modules from the lander. Tom sorted them into boxes of dust, to be kept in the cargo bay, and scavenged electrical components, to go in through the airlock.

By the time he had reentered *Moonstalker*'s living space, Tom found the entire crew clustered around the remote-arm video screen. Sue was moving the arm, with the camera in its end, around the strapped-down crystal.

"Incredible," Packard breathed, staring at the changing facets of the glowing translucence. "What do you make of those structures inside? Could it really be—"

"I think it's a constructed object—not made by human hands," Tom said flatly. "We went out looking for aliens, and we found their calling card. The only problem is, they passed by maybe a hundred million years too early."

He pointed at the boxes of electrical components. "Right now I think this stuff is of more
practical use."

By the time they had finished sorting the
scavenged gear, *Moonstalker* was out from behind the Moon.

"I have an open circuit on a communication satellite," Neal Tyrone reported. "Who's
going to talk to the folks in Houston?"

Chuck Nelson turned to Tom. "I think you've
earned the mike," he said.

In Frederick Napier's Houston office, the
NASA administrator, Mr. Swift, and Rick
Cantwell sat in gloomy silence. It was almost
like a wake.

Outside, Mission Control was humming
along like a well-oiled machine. The computer
virus was history, having been isolated for
study by the computer gurus. The destroyed
terminal had been replaced. Everything was
back to its predisaster self. Except, of course,
that *Moonstalker* had slipped behind the
Moon and never returned.

"We have to face facts," Napier said gravely.
"Our transmitters are back in service, and
they're aimed where *Moonstalker* is supposed
to be. The shuttle should have come out from
behind the Moon hours ago. We've heard
nothing."

He took a deep breath. "I'm sorry, Swift.

The media are beginning to press us. *Moonstalker* has missed two video feeds. Rumors have gotten out about the, ah, disruption at Mission Control. The newspeople smell blood. I can't hold them off much longer."

At that moment, his office monitor flashed into life. Eyes Only Transmission appeared in shocking green letters. Then Tom Swift's face appeared.

The members of the mourning party nearly fell off their chairs.

"Son!" shouted Mr. Swift.

"Tom!" yelled Rick.

"Swift!" Frederick Napier's face turned even redder than ever.

Tom cut through the babble of exclamations to report what had happened behind the Moon.

"Well, the gloves have come off now," Napier said. "I told your father that someone was trying to gut NASA. We thought it would be some subtle sabotage, not an attempt to blow you away."

"That was the fiendish part of it," Tom said. "We'd have crashed hundreds of miles from that pulse generator. It would be just another human tragedy—another NASA failure."

Napier nodded. "Congressional hearings. Protests. No more funding, no more supershuttles."

"But all of NASA's research would be available for somebody else to steal," Tom pointed out. "With a fleet of long-range shuttles, an unscrupulous company—or group of companies—could gain an unbeatable lead in the space race. Our little accident may have been the setup for a land-grab of unbelievable proportions." Tom's face grew very serious. "Somebody is trying very hard to steal space."

"But they haven't succeeded yet," Tom Swift, Sr., said with a hard smile. "What do you expect their next move will be?"

"I think they'll let the negative publicity build and then start pressing for NASA to be dismantled. At the same time, they'll want to display their own space capability," Tom said.

"And show they've got space development all sewed up," Napier growled. The conversation was interrupted by frantic rapping on Napier's office door. Mr. Swift had just enough time to turn the monitor so Tom's face didn't show as a public affairs staffer came rushing in.

"Mr. Napier, there's something on television you've got to see." The young man was sweating so heavily, his horn-rimmed glasses were fogged. "Our phones are already ringing off the hook with requests for comments—"

"Out!" Napier told the staff man as he

turned on the office television. "I'll talk to you when I know what you're talking about."

All the major networks were showing the same image: a squat, heavyset man wearing a spacesuit, standing in front of a forest of microphones. The setting was obviously outdoors, and they could see palm trees in the background.

"Mr. Takashima!" a member of the press corps called out. "Does this mean—"

"Please let me finish my prepared statement," the man on-screen said. "Then I will answer all questions."

Mr. Swift stared stonily at Yuri Takashima's face. "Well, now we know who the villain is. He certainly knows how to put on a show. That spacesuit must be a custom-made job to fit him so well."

As Rick stared at the screen, he realized what Mr. Swift meant. Yuri Takashima showed perfect teeth in a broad smile. His thick, blunt features could hardly be called handsome, but he knew how to address himself to a camera to make himself look good. His eyes and skin color made it clear he was Asian, but the arrangement of his features and heavy mustache made him subtly different.

"My parents made me a citizen of the world," Takashima went on with an obviously well-rehearsed portion of his speech. "My father is Japanese, while my mother came from Russia. Thus you see here a mixture of the questing spirit of the West with the wisdom and patience of the East."

His face now grew serious. "I can understand the search for knowledge and adventure that sent *Moonstalker* forth. Even though, as a businessman, I distrust the romantic notion of searching for mysterious aliens."

Takashima shot a quick smile at the camera, then became grave again. "And as a citizen of the world, I must of course be concerned when a voyage of discovery goes wrong, as apparently the *Moonstalker* mission has. It has been long hours since any news has been heard from the NASA shuttle."

Now Takashima played the leader of men. "However, I promise that the first mission of the shuttle on that launching field over there." He gestured dramatically, and the camera swung to a launching gantry with a tall booster rocket surmounted by a sleek, delta-winged shape.

"That's a revamped Russian space shuttle!" Napier exclaimed.

"I'd heard they might be for sale," Mr. Swift said.

The cameras came back to Takashima. "Yes, the first mission of the *Washi* will be a search, and I hope, a rescue, of the NASA space mission."

Now he oozed sincerity. "It is only right

that we, the representatives of the new world order, should enter the great adventure of space. And it is only fitting that our first flight should be to aid NASA, to help remove the burden from that great organization's shoulders."

"Makes the agency sound like an arthritic oldster," grumped Napier.

"*Washi* is the Japanese word for 'eagle,' " Takashima explained. "So, as this 'eagle' first soars, let us hope its eyes will be sharp enough to find the lost astronauts."

"Now we're incompetent as well as arthritic," Napier said. "If your son hadn't gotten our ship through, this guy would be killing us."

A hand appeared from off-screen, holding out a telephone.

"I am now being connected to NASA's Houston offices, so that I can offer my aid to the head of the *Moonstalker* mission, Mr. Frederick Napier."

Beneath the image, the helpful network news department had superimposed the word *Live.*

At the same moment, Napier's telephone rang. The NASA administrator turned so red, Rick feared his face might explode. "The guy got my personal line!"

Still, when he answered the phone, his voice sounded fairly calm.

Mr. Swift turned down the sound on the

TV, to avoid the confusion of the brief delay between broadcast sound and real life.

"I very much appreciate your generous offer, but I must decline," Napier said. From the look on his face, he intended to spill everything over the phone.

Tom Swift, Sr., waved his arms and gave his head a negative shake.

Napier went on smoothly. "We may be facing some technical problems on the *Moonstalker* mission, but NASA is unwilling to write off our people so quickly."

On the TV screen, Yuri Takashima seemed surprised. "Ah," he said. "Then NASA has another shuttle to send to their aid."

Napier was sweating. Takashima was winning the publicity war. Now NASA was not merely arthritic and incompetent, but heartless. "We, uh, don't have another shuttle ready, but—"

"Then you must accept my offer!" Takashima cut in. "How can you reject the possible rescue of your brave crew?"

"Mr. Takashima," Napier said, smiling at a sudden inspiration, "impressive as your system appears, it is untested. I couldn't encourage you to risk your life on a mission that may not be necessary. Thank you again, and goodbye."

Yuri Takashima's face went from gracious to ugly. "What is NASA trying to hide?" he demanded, slamming the phone down. "For too long, space has been the plaything of the great powers. But it belongs to the world!"

"That is, to him," Mr. Swift said angrily.

"Space is no place for petty political secrets," Takashima declaimed. "It is now open to everyone."

"Everyone who has about a billion dollars handy to build a shuttle," Napier added.

"Perhaps Mr. Napier and NASA hope to discourage the Takashima consortium. Apparently, they would rather let their people die than have them rescued by a shuttle that doesn't fly their flag." Yuri Takashima sneered at the idea. "If so, *they* will be discouraged. *Washi* is already nearing the final two-hour mark before lift-off. My crew and I will soon be boarding."

Now the cameras pulled back to show two other spacesuited figures standing beside Takashima. Tom senior leapt to his feet. "That blond guy on the left—that's Ulrich!" He turned to Napier. "I hope your people are getting a copy of this. We can show it to Allie McVeigh and get a positive ID."

A technician came forward now to whisper in Takashima's ear. The electronics magnate turned to the cameras, his trained image never cracking. "I am afraid I can answer no questions, after all. The countdown progresses perfectly, and we are required aboard."

He waved to the reporters like a conquering hero. "To the *Moonstalker* crew, if you can hear us," he shouted. "Hold on! The *Washi* is lifting!"

ABOARD *MOONSTALKER*, TOM SWIFT FOUGHT TO keep his eyes open. It had been two days since his father had passed on the news of Yuri Takashima's news conference and the launch of the *Washi*. Tom had spent all that time strengthening *Moonstalker*'s computer system, trying to prepare the ship for the voyage home and for any confrontation with the *Washi*.

With his father's help, Tom had convinced Frederick Napier not to release the news that *Moonstalker* and her crew were fine. "The only way we can hope to get the truth out of Takashima is to shake him up," he had argued. "If we surprise him and he loses it, we can record it and have some proof of what he was up to."

As far as the public knew, the supershuttle's mission was in grave jeopardy. Takashima, of course, would believe his plan had succeeded and that *Moonstalker* had crashed. His rescue mission would turn into a new publicity offensive, perhaps showing photos of the downed craft. Tom didn't think the *Washi* was able to land and claim salvage rights.

Soon the *Washi* would come sweeping into lunar orbit. And there was still so much to get ready!

Moonstalker ran on Houston time, and this was the middle of the night. Most of the shuttle crew was sleeping. They just didn't have the knowledge to help Tom build what had to be made.

As he worked on his jury-rigged piece of equipment, the circuits seemed to blur before Tom's eyes. "Have I got it right this time?" he asked tiredly.

Rob the robot ran a trickle current through the apparatus. "It's not the frequency your father gave us."

Tom sighed, blinked his eyes blearily, and got ready for a little more tinkering. "This would be a lot easier if we had the right parts for the job, instead of a bagful of scavenged chips."

"Maybe. But as you remarked, it's a long walk to the nearest Transmitters Iz Us."

By trying different chips and adding filtering circuits, Tom finally succeeded.

"You did it, Tom! This is exactly the frequency your father told us to aim for. You've got to hand it to him. Tom? Tom?"

After the first three words, Tom Swift was dead to the world. Nodding off, a smile on his face, he floated over his handiwork. Rob cut the current running through the patched-together circuit boards.

"I'll wrap this up in a protective box and add the high-power leads," the robot said quietly. Rob rose to his feet, scooped Tom from midair, and steered him to one of the bunks. After lacing Tom into the sleeping facility so he wouldn't float away, Rob returned to the work at hand. "We never sleep," the robot muttered.

Tom enjoyed several hours' sleep until he was shaken by the shoulder. He blinked for a second, then focused on Sue Chong floating in midair beside his bunk.

"Rob said you'd left strict orders to be awakened before we got into *Washi*'s detector range. That will be happening pretty soon," she said. "I hope you have enough tricks up your spacesuit sleeve."

"That makes two of us," Tom admitted, rubbing his eyes. "We'll find out soon enough."

Knowing the trajectory of Takashima's

craft, Tom and Captain Nelson had plotted its most likely course into lunar orbit. Then they had positioned *Moonstalker* to meet the *Washi* on the far side of the Moon. As Tom put it, "If he thinks he's safely in the Moon's radio shadow, maybe Mr. T. will talk turkey."

Moonstalker, with the *Nestor* trailing slightly behind, was orbiting lazily as the *Washi* swung round the Moon and overtook them. Captain Nelson hit his transmit button, sending the message in audio and video. "*Moonstalker* to *Washi*, come in, please. Welcome to Luna!"

Washi's response was also on an AV link. This allowed the supershuttle's crew to see Yuri Takashima's dumbfounded face on their video monitors.

"*M-Moonstalker!*" he managed to get out, taking in the faces of Nelson, Tom, and Sue Chong. "This is the *Washi*, a space vessel of the Takashima Space Consortium, Yuri Takashima commanding. We've come here on a rescue mission, since you haven't been transmitting to Earth."

He glanced cagily at them. "Are you suffering some sort of malfunction—perhaps in your long-range transmission arrays?"

"Actually, Mr. Takashima, we had a worse problem than that," Tom spoke up. "You see, some slimy lowlife suckered us to the dark side of the Moon with a phony alien map."

"Phony, you say?"

"That's right. When we orbited over the section of the Moon indicated on the map, we found a second phony artifact. This one was rigged to knock out all our computers with an electromagnetic pulse."

Takashima did his best to look shocked. "But that would destroy all control aboard your shuttle! What did you do?"

"We were lucky enough to survive," Tom said flatly. "I bet it's a big surprise for you."

"Surprise?" Takashima still tried to act innocent. "I don't underst—"

"We not only survived, we got down to the Moon's surface to examine the artifact," Tom told him. "Don't worry about retrieving it. We took the guts of the machine back up—all those Takashima circuit boards."

"I'm afraid I still don't understand," Takashima insisted.

"Let's just cut to the chase," Tom said. "We found a phony map in orbit—alien-looking symbols carved into a block of stone that obviously came from Earth. We also have a piece of debris from the black-body surveillance satellite sent up with it. Although your spy-eye exploded, a Takashima circuit board got blown my way."

Yuri Takashima now frowned in thought.

"Then there's our mission, which got a lot of media coverage because of this so-called alien map," Tom continued. "And, of course, the booby trap that nearly wrecked us is also made from Takashima components."

"I'm sorry for any problems you experienced, but mine is a very large company. Anyone can buy what we produce." A hiss crept into Yuri Takashima's voice. "If, as you say, there were Takashima components in this so-called artifact, that is of course unfortunate."

His eyes narrowed as he gazed into the camera. "But there is nothing to connect me with any hoax."

"Nice try, Takashima," Tom said. "But the pulse transmitter was made exclusively of Takashima parts. I'd say it had to come from a Takashima lab. In fact, that's exactly what I'll say to every media person on Earth. The evidence might not stand up in a court of law, but then, you're not dealing with the law. You're dealing with public relations. And what people will think of you will be what my father thinks of you—a crook who runs his company like a pirate ship."

Aboard the *Washi*, Yuri Takashima looked offended. "Why, you make me sound like a small-time thief," he complained. "I assure you, the expenditures on this operation were anything but small. There was the hefty fee to the language expert who designed that unearthly numerical script. Then came the costs of polishing and carving my bogus cube in a vacuum chamber. Not to mention the costs of rocketing it into orbit, along with the surveillance satellite."

He shook his head. "*That* was a money-loser. I expected to get additional intelligence on operating a supershuttle. Instead, the satellite self-destructed. And then there was the expense of launching my little automated surprise to the Moon." Takashima smiled for the camera. "No, as a thief, I've never gone in for anything small."

His lips twisted, the smile suddenly gone grim. "As for being a space pirate—well, how's this for starters?"

He flung a command over his shoulder. It wasn't in Japanese, Tom realized, but in Russian.

Takashima's smile was definitely nasty now. "If you don't mind, I'll switch the transmission to our long-range cameras."

His face disappeared from the screen, and the blackness of a starfield appeared before their eyes. The image zoomed in to center on two objects. One was a space shuttle—*Moonstalker*. Above and behind it trailed the empty auxiliary lander, the *Nestor*.

Abruptly, an intense red beam stabbed into the picture. It struck the fuel tank of the *Nestor*. In a silent flare, the lander suddenly disappeared.

Alarms sounded over the loudspeakers as

the shock wave hit the supershuttle. "The *Nestor!*" Tom heard Rob's voice blaring. "It's exploded!"

"We know," Tom assured the robot. "And we know how it was done. That was—"

"A one-gigawatt laser," Takashima said silkily, reappearing on the screen. "Not, of course, part of the standard equipment when I took over this shuttle."

He paused, giving them a sardonic smile. "But I'm sure you'll agree it's just what every aspiring space pirate captain would ask for. Especially if he's confronted with annoying human problems."

Sue Chong stared in fury at the man on the screen. "You don't expect us to take this sitting down, do you?" she demanded.

"I expect you'll 'take' anything I hand out," Takashima informed her coolly. "Because in the end, you, the boy genius, the brave captain, the rest of the crew—and yes, your precious *Moonstalker*—will be scattered atoms. Just like that interesting lunar lander. Ulrich," Takashima went on, glancing over his shoulder, "make a note. You really must steal the plans for that lander system."

He turned back to the screen. "How unfortunate for you that this little confrontation took place *behind* the Moon, where radio transmissions can't possibly reach Earth." Takashima smiled as if he'd just been told a wonderful joke. "And though I'm sure you're recording everything I say, those tapes will never reach Earth, either."

The smile disappeared. "As far as the media is concerned—and I've spent a good deal of money spreading the rumors—*Moonstalker* has crashed and exploded. And we can't disappoint the media, can we? Especially when NASA has said nothing about your fates."

Again Yuri Takashima glanced coolly over his shoulder. "Ulrich, has the laser recharged yet? Excellent."

Smiling into the screen, he said, "Target *Moonstalker*, Ulrich . . . and destroy it."

ALL CREW MEMBERS STRAP IN!" CAPTAIN Chuck Nelson shouted. "I'm going to attempt evasive maneuvers!" Nelson's blue eyes were cold as steel as he reached for his command console.

Aboard the *Washi*, Yuri Takashima began to laugh. A mocking smile twisted his blunt-featured face. "Do you really believe your shuttle can outrun the speed of light, Captain?" he asked. "I think my *Eagle*'s grasp far exceeds your engines' reach."

Tom knew that there was no escape from the *Washi*'s laser cannon. But he also knew that Chuck Nelson was only acting, keeping Takashima's attention so that Tom could try a desperate plan. From his seat in the copilot's chair, Tom was also transmitting—on the spacesuit-radio circuit.

There was a reason that Nelson, Sue, and Tom were the only ones on the flight deck. The rest of the crew were suited up and positioned in the cargo bay at various action stations. "Now!" Tom yelled.

Sue darted to the aft control panel. "They've started!" she said, looking out through the rear windows.

Tom gripped the arms of his seat. Either his plan would work, or they'd all get fried. Through the front windows of the shuttle, he saw little white crystals come floating past. It was almost like watching the first snowfall of winter.

The tiny white grains danced in front of the windows, becoming more and more numerous. Now they seemed to form a fog, growing thicker and thicker, until it appeared that *Moonstalker* was flying through a cloud.

But Tom knew what that cloud was composed of and how it had come about. The cloud was the work of Neal Tyrone, Professor Packard, and Professor Domovoy. Tethered in the cargo bay, they'd unsealed certain cargo modules brought over from the now-destroyed *Nestor*. The chests had been filled with the glowing dust crystals Tom and Rob had found on the Moon.

The storage boxes had been filled with

something else while *Moonstalker* had waited for the *Washi* to arrive. Crew members had pumped in air. When they had unsealed the boxes at Tom's command, the air had whooshed out into the vacuum of space. The crystals had also been carried along, to whirl around *Moonstalker*.

Actually, Professor Packard had given Tom the idea. "It's amazing how reflective those little dust grains are," he had said. "They keep breaking up my spectrographic laser."

When Tom had heard that, he'd immediately started formulating plans. He knew that they'd need defenses to confront the *Washi*—but had he made the right decision?

Glancing at the communications video screen, Tom could barely make out Takashima's face. Snow and interference covered the screen. Another result of the cloud around them, Tom realized. The dust grains didn't just break up light. They also broke up radio and television signals.

Although the audio was static-filled and wobbly, Tom could still make out the anger in Yuri Takashima's voice. "What are you doing? Ulrich! *Fire!*"

Tom tensed in his seat. There was no way of telling where the laser blast was aimed. *Moonstalker*'s exterior cameras were blinded by the protective dust cloud.

Everyone knew when the laser was fired,

though. The whole dust cloud turned pink, a lovely rosy color like sunrise on a spring day.

"It worked!" Tom breathed as the cloud faded, then grew pink again. "The shiny facets on those little crystals deflect and reflect the laser beam millions of times. And each time, the beam gets spread out a little more."

"So the result is a pretty pink light show instead of a destructive bolt of concentrated energy." Captain Chuck Nelson relaxed a little in his command chair. "I've got to hand it to you, kid. I wasn't so sure this stunt would work."

"That makes two of us," Tom admitted.

He took a deep breath and faced the video transmission pickup. "Looks like your *Eagle*'s claws got lost in the fog, Takashima. That makes two strikes at trying to kill us. You laughed before about being a pirate. Now we have the first taped proof of an act of space piracy. You might as well give up."

Takashima looked amused. "And how do you expect me to do that? Am I supposed to surrender my ship?"

"I expect you to *abandon* your ship," Tom told him coolly. "One of your men can wear a spacesuit. The others will have to come out in space-rescue bags. I assume those are standard equipment aboard your craft."

Space-rescue bags were a combination lifeboat and emergency spacesuit. They were about the size of a large garbage bag, with an air supply and radio beacon but no helmet or window. Being zipped into one of those things had been a major low point in Tom's astronaut training. He'd crouched in the dark, uncomfortably pent in, wondering how long the test would last. It was the closest he'd ever come to claustrophobia. But what he had hated most of all was the feeling of utter helplessness in that little bubble of air. Before Tom dealt with Yuri Takashima face-to-face, he wanted the rogue industrialist as helpless as possible.

Takashima sat back in his command chair, pretending to consider Tom's demand. But the smile on his face showed that he was only pretending. Obviously, he still thought he had the upper hand in this confrontation.

"You mentioned before that I already had two strikes at killing you," Takashima finally said. "Well, I do not share the same interest most Japanese have in baseball. But even I know that I have three strikes before I'm out."

His smile showed no amusement. "We're still hidden behind the Moon and will be for a good hour yet. And I still have my laser. I don't believe you have the capacity for long-distance transmission, or you'd have told the world about your survival long ago. Thus I believe I am still master of this situation."

"We didn't tell the world about our survival because we didn't want to warn you that we'd be here," Tom shot back. "We figured rightly that this was the only way to force you into the open. You'd be sure to mount a phony rescue operation to show off your new shuttle." Tom looked steadily into the camera pickup. "But you'd better know this, Takashima. NASA knew we were alive two days ago. We told them everything on a secure communications link."

Takashima's image on the screen stared hard at him. Then the *Washi*'s commander sat back in his chair. "I don't believe you," he said finally. "I think you are trying to pull a bluff. But it won't work, Swift. Sooner or later, you'll have to take *Moonstalker* back to Earth. When you do, you'll have to leave that protective cloud, whatever it is. And my laser will have you targeted."

"All we have to do is make it to the other side of the Moon," Tom snapped. "Then you'll see who can broadcast or not."

"A desperate bluff." Takashima made a dismissing gesture with his hand. "Even if your long-range transmission array were in perfect order—which I doubt—you couldn't send a message to Earth."

He pointed a finger at Tom. "That dust cloud weakens your communications signals so badly, they can barely reach *me*. And I'm only fifty miles away. Don't make empty threats at me, Swift. As for expecting me to surrender . . ."

Yuri Takashima gave Tom a sneering smile. "I think the children in your country say, 'Make me.' "

Now it was Tom Swift's turn to smile humorlessly. "Okay, Takashima. Just remember, you asked for it."

He tapped the Transmit button on the spacesuit-radio frequency. "Rob, we've asked Takashima to surrender, but he won't unless we make him." Tom took a deep breath. "So make him."

"Are you sure this will work?" Chuck Nelson asked nervously. "I mean, a lot of the electronics on this baby are held together with baling wire and spit. How do you know your little electronic warfare gadget won't knock us out, too?"

"We'll know in a second," Tom said. The lights around them dimmed as the ship's energy was drained for a moment. "That should do it."

Tom got back on the spacesuit frequency. "Okay, Rob. Take off and check them out."

"I hope your gadget works as advertised," Rob's voice came back over the radio. "Laser beams are bad for my complexion."

Tom knew that Rob had been waiting in the cargo bay, an MMU strapped to his back.

This was the bulky NASA model, with a video camera clipped to the top of the harness. "I'm out of the cloud," Rob reported. "Transmitting video—now!"

Another monitor popped to life aboard the shuttle. This one showed a sprinkling of stars against the inky blackness of deep space. A blurred form floated in the foreground. As Rob jetted closer, the focus improved.

The form resolved itself into a space shuttle, shiny new, with a red-and-white color scheme on its heat-resistant tiles and a large Takashima logo on its wings and tail.

"Well, they haven't zapped me yet," Rob radioed.

"Rob, aim for the windows," Tom ordered.

"Will do, Tom." The image on the screen shifted, blurred, then expanded as Rob aimed the camera and focused on the *Washi*'s flight deck windows.

They were dark.

"Looks like my gadget went beyond the call," Tom said softly.

"I just wanted to give them a taste of what they did to us. So I rewired the electromagnetic pulse generator from the phony lunar artifact to send out a pulse on Takashima's computer frequency." Tom smiled grimly. "That was a bit of information my dad was happy to supply."

The smile faded as he stared at the apparently derelict craft in the screen. "I didn't expect Takashima to bring his shuttle so close to us. It looks like the pulse did a lot more than knock their computers out."

Tom's voice was tight. "It looks like it left them with no power at all."

AFTER A LONG LOOK AT THE LIGHTLESS *WASHI*,
Tom called Rob back to the *Moonstalker*.

"What's up, Tom?" the robot asked after
coming through the airlock. The stark cold of
space radiated off Rob's metal skin.

"I want your MMU completely charged
up," Tom said. "You'll also need some special
supplies: a pen, paper, and, I think, a flashlight."

Rob's metal face couldn't indicate puzzlement, but the flash of his photoelectric eyes
did almost as well. "What for?"

"We're going to recommence communication with the *Washi*." Tom pointed to the
communications monitor, which was a hash
of static.

"They've gone off the air. I think we'd better accept Takashima's surrender before he runs out of air."

Rob found an easy way to open negotiations. He jetted over to the stricken shuttlecraft, rapped on the flight deck window, then shone the light inside. Communication was by written notes, pressed against the window. Rob relayed Takashima's messages to Tom by radio, then Tom radioed responses for Rob to write down.

"Looks like Takashima's taken a pretty big fall," Chuck Nelson said with a grin. "From lasers to crayons, in one simple lesson."

The crew of the *Washi* was frantic. All power had been lost. Nothing worked at all, including the air pumps. If they didn't abandon ship soon, the crew would end up choking on their own used air.

Still Takashima tried to haggle. Rob was kept busy shifting paper, pen, and the flashlight around. "Hey, Tom," he said over the radio at one point. "Next time we sit down at the old drawing board, what say we design some pockets for me?"

In the end, Takashima had no negotiating room, nowhere to wriggle. Tom absolutely refused to attempt to save the *Washi*. "We barely have enough components to keep *us* going," he told Takashima. "Where are we going to find the equipment to repair your ship?"

Tom also had to explain that there was no way *Moonstalker* could boost the *Washi* to a safer orbit. Takashima's shuttle would have to remain in its decaying orbital pattern until it crashed into the Moon's surface.

"This guy may be a hotshot businessman," Chuck Nelson said, listening to Rob relay Takashima's pleas. "But as an astronaut, he doesn't know his elbow from a hole in the ground. What does he expect us to do, tie a rope around his ship and tow it home for him?"

More serious were the arrangements for evacuating the crew from the *Washi*. With the failure of all systems, the pumps and electronic doors of the airlock wouldn't work. Rob was lucky to find tools in the *Washi*'s open cargo bay. He'd use those to break in. But before he cracked the door, he had to make sure the crew members were suited up, or in their rescue bags.

"Okay," Rob radioed at long last. "They say they're all zipped up and strapped in."

Tom had insisted that the crew members and everything else movable be secured before the rescue attempt. When Rob broke the seal on the inside airlock door, all the atmosphere aboard the *Washi* would be sucked into space. The air would rush out the door at near-hurricane force. Anything loose would come flying with it.

The creak of bending metal came over the radio, transmitted to Rob's receiver through the metal of his body. Then "Whoa!" Rob yelled. "We've got a bit of a breeze here. Those guys could have done a better job of tidying up. All sorts of junk is flying past. Lucky thing I tethered myself before I began this job."

Finally, however, Rob was able to report that he was inside the flight deck. "Takashima is strapped into a chair. He's pointing at two rescue bags, also strapped in. I've got one now, he's got the other, and we're heading for the airlock."

Once in the *Washi*'s cargo bay, Takashima took the rescue bubbles, one in each hand. Rob clamped his metal legs around the industrialist's legs and triggered the jets on the MMU. Soon they were coming in for a landing at *Moonstalker*'s cargo bay.

The NASA crew was already inside the supershuttle, their business in the cargo bay finished. Nelson and Tyrone had accelerated the shuttle out of the dust cloud, bringing *Moonstalker* closer to the stricken craft. They were almost out of the Moon's radio shadow. Soon they could announce their safety to the world and head home.

Tom and the others stood on the middeck

level, waiting for the airlock to cycle. Although larger than the one in the original shuttle, it was barely roomy enough for three people. Rob would have to wait his turn outside, by the entrance to the cargo bay.

The airlock's inner hatch opened, and Yuri Takashima stumbled out. He pulled the two escape bubbles after him, then gave them two hearty slaps.

It's a code, Tom realized, to let the people inside know they've reached safety.

Takashima undid his helmet and glanced around at the crew members. The escape bags floated in midair, bulging and jumping as if they were alive. The zipper gave on one, and out came an Asian crewman, pale-faced and gasping.

Then the second bag opened, and Ulrich emerged. As the slim German came out of his crouch, he revealed something in his hand— a 9-mm pistol.

"No one is to move," he said coldly.

"So now you're going to try to hijack us?" Tom said in disbelief. "Have you completely lost your mind, Takashima? How are you going to explain this?"

"I don't know right now, and I don't care," Yuri Takashima grated in reply. "I'll worry about that problem after I've gotten rid of you."

He took a deep breath, calming himself

down. "Perhaps I'll cannibalize your equipment to get my ship running again. Or perhaps I'll go home in your ship—with a suitably bizarre story for the press, of course." He made wide gestures, as if he were laying out a headline. " 'The *Moonstalker* Mystery—Damaged Shuttle Found Empty of Crew.' You could become an interesting segment on those unsolved-crime TV shows."

Takashima's eyes gleamed with hate as he stared at Tom. "I'm afraid you'll never know, Swift. You, the copilot, and the lovely Ms. Chong will be the first to go out the airlock. As your blood boils away, you can remember that Yuri Takashima never loses."

Ulrich had now maneuvered himself so that he was against a wall, aiming down at them. "Move!" he barked, gesturing to the airlock with his pistol.

Fast as a bullet, Chuck Nelson bounced off the floor to ram into Ulrich. The hired gun gave a loud "Oof!" as Nelson caught him in the belly. They both bounced off the wall together, Ulrich struggling to aim the pistol and Nelson nimbly slipping around to put a choke hold on him.

Takashima tried to jump into the fight, but Tom rammed into him. Packard and Domovoy also leapt on the industrialist, while Neal Tyrone went to Nelson's aid.

The captain didn't need it. He had Ulrich's

gun in one hand as he restrained the limply floating agent with an armlock round the neck.

"Microgravity martial arts," he said with a grin. "A couple of guys and I invented the sport on our last few missions."

"Lucky thing," Tom said. "I'd hate to think what would have happened if that gun had gone off in here."

Nelson shuddered. "Me, too. That's why I had to nail that clown—and fast."

Yuri Takashima struggled and swore as the *Moonstalker*'s crew tied him up. Ulrich was still unconscious. The third *Washi* crew-member didn't resist. He just huddled down, his head in his hands.

As the prisoners were stowed away on the middeck, Tom and Captain Nelson climbed upstairs. "Here's the mike," Nelson said, checking the automatic pilot. "We're free to call Earth."

Tom pressed the Transmit button. "Mission Control, this is *Moonstalker*. We're fine, we're coming home, and boy, have we got a story to tell you. I'm just glad it's all on tape, because this will be a tough one to believe."

Two days later, the supershuttle swept down to a perfect landing at Edwards Air Force Base. The crew members were strapped into their seats. The prisoners were tied and

laced into the bunk beds. Besides the usual
technicians who swept over the shuttle,
Moonstalker was met by a team of FBI agents.
Swearing in several languages, Takashima
was led away.

There was also a special welcoming com-
mittee. The vice president was there, along
with the head of NASA, a couple of U.S. senators, and, of course, Frederick Napier. All
Tom noticed was the small group off to the
side—his father, his mother, his sister, Sandra, Rick, and Mandy Coster.

After a few weeks of headlines and press
conferences, the media uproar finally died
down. The press people hadn't minded losing
their big space disaster story after the tapes
of Takashima's attempted space piracy got
out. They gave the full front-page treatment
to the discussions on where the trial should
take place and to the shenanigans of Takashima's lawyers. "Is space piracy the same thing
as air piracy?" one of these legal minds
inquired.

Mr. Swift wasn't impressed by this reason-
ing. "I think Takashima has less to worry
about from the law than he does from his consortium partners."

"What do you mean?" Tom asked.

"They put untold millions of dollars into
this space-grab," Mr. Swift pointed out. "And

what do they have to show for it? Takashima even lost their spacecraft."

"*Washi*," Rick Cantwell said with a chuckle. "More like wash*out*, if you ask me."

Alison McVeigh was less lucky. For destroying federal property, she could look forward to a prison sentence, even if she got leniency from the court for testifying against Ulrich.

Soon enough, however, *Moonstalker* mania became an old story.

One part of the story that the media never received, however, was the discovery of the strange crystal in Hertzsprung Crater. NASA had quickly sworn the crew and Tom Swift, Sr., to secrecy. Tom had given up ever knowing more about the artifact, when Professor Packard turned up at Swift Enterprises.

Tom entered his father's office to find the professor looking a lot more tired than he had ever seen him before. Even Packard's plump pink cheeks sagged a little. "NASA figured on keeping things in the 'need to know' family, so I was given the job of examining the crystal," he explained. "I've x-rayed it, run current through it, poked it, even looked at it through a scanning, tunneling microscope." He shook his head. "All the while keeping the blasted thing in a vacuum chamber."

"And what have you learned?" Mr. Swift asked.

"Nothing," Packard admitted bitterly. "Now I'm supposed to take the crystal out of vacuum and examine it even more exhaustively. Frankly, I need help and a good facility. And since you're also among those in the 'need to know' category, I'm turning to you."

Tom turned eagerly to his father. "This is something we *have* to do."

Tom senior smiled. "Took the words right out of my mouth, son."

The vacuum-sealed crystal arrived by truck three days later. That evening Packard, Tom, and Mr. Swift gathered in a testing vault. Tom and his father were already wearing sterilized "clean suits" and had one ready for the professor.

As Packard donned his suit, he stared at the equipment surrounding the lab bench. "When you propose to test something, Swift, you certainly go all-out. Obviously, you're prepared for procedures I hadn't even thought about."

"It's best to be ready for everything," Tom's father said. He started the recording cameras. "Shall we unseal the crystal now?"

Packard's deft fingers went to the clear acrylic plastic box containing the crystal. He touched a fitting, and with a loud pop of incoming air, the box opened.

"Now, let's see how it feels," Packard said expectantly. But he gasped as his gloved hands reached for the crystal. Its pale gleam became brighter and brighter. For a moment, the strange structures inside the huge gem seemed to be outlined in blazing light. Then, as the room filled with an eerie blue glow, the crystal seemed to shrink in on itself and disappear.

Or was it shrinking? Tom remembered another time he had seen that cold blue, blinding light. That had been on the event horizon of a black hole.

There was another audible pop of air filling vacuum. Then, as they blinked away the fierce afterimage burnt into their eyes, the three men found themselves staring at an empty lab bench.

"Nothing—gone!" Packard exclaimed. "That radiance. What was it?"

"A space-warp, perhaps?" Tom's father suggested.

"It's hard to offer a hypothesis with so little evidence, but think of this," Tom suggested. "The crystal was left on the side of the Moon facing away from the Earth in near-vacuum. If intelligent life were to appear on Earth, sooner or later it—we—would reach the Moon. And what would we do with the artifact? Bring it back to Earth and into Earth's atmosphere."

"So you're suggesting the crystal is some

sort of intelligence-alerting device?" Mr. Swift asked.

Tom shrugged. "I don't know what it is. But that's one theory that seems to fit the facts."

"So whoever or whatever planted that crystal millions of years ago will now be receiving a message that there's intelligent life on the third planet of the star Sol," Packard said softly.

"Perhaps," Mr. Swift responded. "If those who planted the crystal haven't become extinct after all this time."

Tom Swift still stared at the spot where the crystal had disappeared. "You know, Dad, now I'll have to throw away one of my favorite T-shirts."

His father turned in surprise. "What?"

Tom shrugged. "You know, the one with the message that says there's no intelligent life here."

He shook his head in wonder. "I think it's just become obsolete."

Tom's next adventure:

Tom Swift has developed a powerful new kind of nanotechnology—incredible shrinking robots reduced to the size of a pinpoint with his revolutionary molecular compressor. But the tiniest miscalculation can have gigantic consequences, as Tom soon finds out for himself. One moment he's running an experiment—and the next he's running for his life!

Zapped by the molecular beam, Tom and his friends are thrust into a miniature but deadly world. A squadron of bees and an army of ants look to make short work—and fast food—out of the bite-size band. But their most dangerous enemy of all is the ticking clock. The condition may soon become irreversible, and time, like everything else, is shrinking fast . . . in Tom Swift #8, *The Microbots*.

HAVE YOU SEEN
THE HARDY BOYS® LATELY?
THE HARDY BOYS™ CASE FILES

- ☐ #1 DEAD ON TARGET .... 73992-1/$3.50
- ☐ #2 EVIL, INC. .... 73668-X/$3.50
- ☐ #3 CULT OF CRIME ...... 68726-3/$2.95
- ☐ #4 THE LAZARUS PLOT .... 73995-6/$3.50
- ☐ #5 EDGE OF DESTRUCTION .... 73669-8/$3.50
- ☐ #6 THE CROWNING TERROR .... 73670-1/$3.50
- ☐ #7 DEATHGAME .... 73993-8/$3.50
- ☐ #8 SEE NO EVIL .... 73673-6/$3.50
- ☐ #9 THE GENIUS THIEVES .... 73767-4/$3.50
- ☐ #10 HOSTAGES OF HATE .... 69579-7/$2.95
- ☐ #11 BROTHER AGAINST BROTHER .... 74391-0/$3.50
- ☐ #12 PERFECT GETAWAY .... 73675-2/$3.50
- ☐ #13 THE BORGIA DAGGER .... 73676-0/$3.50
- ☐ #14 TOO MANY TRAITORS .... 73677-9/$3.50
- ☐ #15 BLOOD RELATIONS .... 68779-4/$2.95
- ☐ #16 LINE OF FIRE ...... 68805-7/$2.95
- ☐ #17 THE NUMBER FILE ... 68806-5/$2.95
- ☐ #18 A KILLING IN THE MARKET .... 68472-8/$2.95
- ☐ #19 NIGHTMARE IN ANGEL CITY .... 69185-6/$2.95
- ☐ #20 WITNESS TO MURDER .... 69434-0/$2.95
- ☐ #21 STREET SPIES .... 69186-4/$2.95
- ☐ #22 DOUBLE EXPOSURE .... 69376-X/$2.95
- ☐ #23 DISASTER FOR HIRE .... 70491-5/$2.95
- ☐ #24 SCENE OF THE CRIME .... 69377-8/$2.95
- ☐ #25 THE BORDERLINE CASE .... 72452-5/$2.95
- ☐ #26 TROUBLE IN THE PIPELINE .... 74661-8/$3.50
- ☐ #27 NOWHERE TO RUN .... 64690-7/$2.95

- ☐ #28 COUNTDOWN TO TERROR .... 74662-6/$3.50
- ☐ #29 THICK AS THIEVES ... 74663-4/$3.50
- ☐ #30 THE DEADLIEST DARE .... 74613-8/$3.50
- ☐ #31 WITHOUT A TRACE .... 74664-2/$3.50
- ☐ #32 BLOOD MONEY ...... 74665-0/$3.50
- ☐ #33 COLLISION COURSE .... 74666-9/$3.50
- ☐ #34 FINAL CUT .... 74667-7/$3.50
- ☐ #35 THE DEAD SEASON .... 74105-5/$3.50
- ☐ #36 RUNNING ON EMPTY .... 74107-1/$3.50
- ☐ #37 DANGER ZONE ...... 73751-1/$3.50
- ☐ #38 DIPLOMATIC DECEIT .... 74106-3/$3.50
- ☐ #39 FLESH AND BLOOD .... 73913-1/$3.50
- ☐ #40 FRIGHT WAVE .... 73994-8/$3.50
- ☐ #41 HIGHWAY ROBBERY .... 70038-3/$2.95
- ☐ #42 THE LAST LAUGH .... 74614-6/$3.50
- ☐ #43 STRATEGIC MOVES .... 70040-5/$2.95
- ☐ #44 CASTLE FEAR ...... 74615-4/$3.50
- ☐ #45 IN SELF-DEFENSE .... 70042-1/$2.95
- ☐ #46 FOUL PLAY .... 70043-X/$2.95
- ☐ #47 FLIGHT INTO DANGER .... 70044-8/$3.50
- ☐ #48 ROCK 'N' REVENGE .... 70033-2/$3.50
- ☐ #49 DIRTY DEEDS ...... 70046-4/$3.50
- ☐ #50 POWER PLAY .... 70047-2/$3.50
- ☐ #51 CHOKE HOLD ...... 70048-0/$3.50
- ☐ #52 UNCIVIL WAR ...... 70049-9/$3.50
- ☐ #53 WEB OF HORROR .... 73089-4/$3.50
- ☐ #54 DEEP TROUBLE .... 73090-8/$3.50
- ☐ #55 BEYOND THE LAW ... 73091-6/$3.50
- ☐ #56 HEIGHT OF DANGER .... 73092-4/$3.50
- ☐ #57 TERROR ON TRACK .... 73093-2/$3.50
- ☐ #58 SPIKED! .... 73094-0/$3.50
- ☐ #59 OPEN SEASON .... 73095-9/$3.50

Simon & Schuster, Mail Order Dept. ASD
200 Old Tappan Rd., Old Tappan, N.J. 07675

Please send me the books I have checked above. I am enclosing $_____ (please add 75¢ to cover postage and handling for each order. Please add appropriate local sales tax). Send check or money order—no cash or C.O.D.'s please. Allow up to six weeks for delivery. For purchases over $10.00 you may use VISA: card number, expiration date and customer signature must be included.

Name _____

Address _____

City _____ State/Zip _____

VISA Card No. _____ Exp. Date _____

Signature _____

120-46

SUPER HIGH TECH ... SUPER HIGH SPEED ... SUPER HIGH STAKES!

TOM SWIFT

VICTOR APPLETON

He's daring, he's resourceful, he's cool under fire. He's Tom Swift, the brilliant teen inventor racing toward the cutting edge of high-tech adventure.

Tom has his own lab, his own robots, his own high-tech playground at Swift Enterprises, a fabulous research lab in California where every new invention is an invitation to excitement and danger.

☐ **TOM SWIFT 1 THE BLACK DRAGON** .... 67823-X/$2.95

☐ **TOM SWIFT 2 THE NEGATIVE ZONE** .... 67824-8/$2.95

☐ **TOM SWIFT 3 CYBORG KICKBOXER** .... 67825-6/$2.95

☐ **TOM SWIFT 4 THE DNA DISASTER** .... 67826-4/$2.95

☐ **TOM SWIFT 5 MONSTER MACHINE** .... 67827-2/$2.99

☐ **TOM SWIFT 6 AQUATECH WARRIORS** ...... 67828-0/$2.99

Simon & Schuster Mail Order Dept. VAA
200 Old Tappan Rd., Old Tappan, N.J. 07675

Please send me the books I have checked above. I am enclosing $_____ (please add 75¢ to cover postage and handling for each order. Please add appropriate local sales tax). Send check or money order—no cash or C.O.D.'s please. Allow up to six weeks for delivery. For purchases over $10.00 you may use VISA: card number, expiration date and customer signature must be included.

Name _____

Address _____

City _____ State/Zip _____

VISA Card No. _____ Exp. Date _____

Signature _____ 246-05

NANCY DREW® AND THE HARDY BOYS®
TEAM UP FOR MORE MYSTERY... MORE THRILLS...AND MORE EXCITEMENT THAN EVER BEFORE!

A NANCY DREW & HARDY BOYS
SuperMystery
by Carolyn Keene

In the NANCY DREW AND HARDY BOYS SuperMystery, Nancy's unique sleuthing and Frank and Joe's hi-tech action-packed approach make for a dynamic combination you won't want to miss!

☐ **DOUBLE CROSSING** 74616-2/$3.50
☐ **A CRIME FOR CHRISTMAS** 74617-0/$3.50
☐ **SHOCK WAVES** 74393-7/$3.50
☐ **DANGEROUS GAMES** 74108-X/$3.50
☐ **THE LAST RESORT** 67461-7/$3.50
☐ **THE PARIS CONNECTION** 74675-8/$3.50
☐ **BURIED IN TIME** 67463-3/$2.95
☐ **MYSTERY TRAIN** 67464-1/$2.95
☐ **BEST OF ENEMIES** 67465-X/$3.50
☐ **HIGH SURVIVAL** 67466-8/$3.50
☐ **NEW YEAR'S EVIL** 67467-6/$3.99

Simon & Schuster Mail Order Dept. NHS
200 Old Tappan Rd., Old Tappan, N.J. 07675

Please send me the books I have checked above. I am enclosing $_____ (please add 75¢ to cover postage and handling for each order. Please add appropriate local sales tax). Send check or money order–no cash or C.O.D.'s please. Allow up to six weeks for delivery. For purchases over $10.00 you may use VISA: card number, expiration date and customer signature must be included.

Name _____

Address _____

City _____ State/Zip _____

VISA Card No. _____ Exp. Date _____

Signature _____ 150-15